Delia stared at his face. His skin was a deep, weathered tan, and his hair hung in heavy thatches around his ears, as though it had been hacked off in chunks with a straight blade. His mouth was wide and thin beneath a straight, narrow nose, and his cheekbones were flat, triangular slabs. He was so thin that the tendons in his neck and forearms sprang out under his skin. Delia's hand shook as she reached out for the knife, half expecting him to clutch at her arm and drag her from the path. She snatched the knife back and, in that instant, recognized him.

"Isaac!"

"Go away. You don't belong here. Go home."

"Isaac, wait." Image tumbled upon image in Delia's mind, past and present, real and remembered, colliding chaotically. Although he wore the same heavy green-and-black plaid shirt and khaki pants, this Isaac was hardly the earnest boy she had known. Crouched on her hands and knees, she stared at him, confused and shaken by his transformation. "Isaac, it's me, Delia."

"Go away. It's not safe here." There was no glimmer of recognition in his tone or expression, no apparent interest in her. She might have been a total stranger, as unfamiliar to him now as he was to her. "You must leave."

JAN O'DONNELL KLAVENESS is the author of several books for young adults, including *The Griffin Legacy*, nominated for the Edgar Allan Poe Award for Children's Books and available in a Dell Laurel-Leaf edition. Ms. Klaveness lives in Hempstead, New York.

ALSO AVAILABLE IN LAUREL-LEAF BOOKS:

GHOST ISLAND.

JAN O'DONNELL KLAVENESS

LAUREL-LEAF BOOKS bring together under a single imprint outstanding works of fiction and nonfiction particularly suitable for young adult readers, both in and out of the classroom. Charles F. Reasoner, Professor Emeritus of Children's Literature and Reading, New York University, is consultant to this series.

Published by
Dell Publishing Co., Inc.
1 Dag Hammarskjold Plaza
New York, New York 10017

Laurel-Leaf Library ® TM 766734, Dell Publishing Co., Inc.

ISBN: 0-440-93097-9

RL: 6.0

Reprinted by arrangement with Macmillan Publishing Company

Printed in the United States of America

December 1987

10 9 8 7 6 5 4 3 2 1

WFH

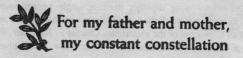

For my father and mother,
my constant constellation

Once the realization is accepted that even between the closest human beings infinite distances continue to exist, a wonderful living side by side can grow up, if they succeed in loving the distance between them, which makes it possible for each to see the other whole and against a wide sky!

—Rainer Maria Rilke
Letters of Rainer Maria Rilke,
1892–1910

GHOST ISLAND

ONE

The lake country appeared unchanged, but Delia Pearce frowned intently out the car window, bracing herself for any alteration in the familiar landmarks along the road. Crossing the border into Canada on the last leg of the journey had always been a disappointment. Delia had never been able to rid herself of the notion that on the far side of customs was a country radically, even magically, different from her own. At fifteen she no longer believed in magic, but as a small child she had imagined a fantastic landscape of technicolored mountains and apricot plains. On her first trip north, as her father drove across the bridge between the two countries, she had strained to see through car windows dim with dawn. When nothing had changed, nothing except the color of the highway from the black macadam of International Falls, Minnesota, to the white asphalt of Fort Frances, Ontario, Delia had been bitterly disappointed.

Now, ten years later, she willed this to be the one place where nothing had changed in the three years since everything had changed.

"How are you doing back there, Delia?" Breaking into the steady hum of the tires on the hot pavement, her mother's voice sounded thin and stiff, but resolutely cheerful. "You're awfully quiet."

"I'm fine. Just hot." Easing forward against the tension of her seat belt, Delia peered over her mother's shoulder at the odometer, clocking the distance they had covered since breakfast. Her skin stuck to the vinyl upholstery of the Toyota no matter how she moved, pulling away and reattaching itself with inescapable suction. "I wish we'd brought the other car," she muttered.

"The other car's not air-conditioned," her mother replied, glancing from the road to Delia's stepfather, who was sitting in the passenger seat next to her. She looked back at Delia in the rearview mirror. The warning muscle twitched in her jaw. "We thought we'd all be more comfortable in Jim's car, cooler and quieter with the windows closed and the air conditioning on."

"What air conditioning? It sure doesn't get to the back seat. At least the other car has fabric upholstery. I can't seem to get unstuck from this plastic stuff." Delia flopped back into her corner.

"Don't forget that this trip was your idea." Her mother's voice sharpened.

"It's just that it was never this hot before," Delia said quickly.

"It isn't usually this hot at dawn, which is when we always crossed the border. Your father was one for driving all night, remember?"

"Sounds like a good idea to me," Delia commented. She waited a moment, but her mother didn't respond. "How much farther is it?"

"Some things never change." Maggie looked into the rearview mirror again, this time offering her daughter a bright smile. "This is just about where you'd start asking, 'Are we there yet?' when we still had a good fifty miles to go. Consider yourself lucky, Jim, that you missed that stage of Delia's life."

"Missing any stage isn't what I'd call luck." Delia's stepfather reached down between the front bucket seats where Delia had jammed her feet in an effort to stretch out her legs. His strong, bony hand closed around the toe of her tennis shoe in a friendly squeeze. "I don't like the vinyl, either," he said, "but it was all I could get. I'll bet you feel permanently bonded to the stuff after two days of riding back there. Want to change places?"

"I'm okay." She withdrew her foot, ostensibly to bend her knees and ankles and to exercise the stiffness out of her joints. Jim let her go and did not press the seating arrangements. Delia resumed her cramped position at the window. "I'm just ready to get there."

The yearning for it closed her throat, welling up unexpectedly. She wanted desperately to be back at the lake, to be there on her island now, in the instant of thinking of it. But she pushed the wanting away, squeezed it back into a hard, tight knot. Squinting into the fierce summer noon, she concentrated on the flat stretches of the Rainy River that bordered the road. So far, everything looked the same. The straight, two-lane highway led north, slipping through small, weather-weary towns and the rain-flooded marshes of the river to the lake. There was more traffic than she remembered, which probably accounted for the unusual number of patrol cars she'd observed. The check at customs had been meticulously thorough, stopping travelers on both sides of the border in long, hot and dusty lines. It hadn't always been like that, not on her first trips to the lake. Delia smiled, remembering. Going back along the familiar route jogged nearly forgotten images, reeling out in her mind scenes from time past like clips from an old film.

"But what's wrong?" her mother asked, trying to console the wailing five-year-old Delia as they drove through the unremarkable landscape on the other side of the bridge between the countries. "What happened?"

Delia wasn't able to explain. She wasn't hungry, she wasn't tired, she wasn't carsick. She hadn't forgotten that they would soon be boating and fishing and swimming at the lake.

"If you keep yowling like that," her father said finally, "you'll scare away the bears and wolves."

Delia's tears subsided at the thought. "And the lions and tigers?" she asked.

"You've frightened them away already," he said. "They're gone."

Maggie laughed. "Don't, Fred. You'll have her terrified."

"Nothing left to be terrified of." Fred Pearce moved his pipe to the other side of his mouth and looked down at his daughter. Like her own, his eyes were brown with glints of green, shadowed as he glanced over his pipe toward her. "All those animals heard you coming and cleared out. Probably nothing left but a few Indians."

"Indians? Wild Indians?"

"That depends on the individual, I suppose." He struck a match and held it over the bowl of his pipe, drawing on it until puffs of smoke filled the car. "They aren't like the ones you see in the movies. They dress like us and live in regular houses."

Delia's chin quivered at the loss of war bonnets and tepees. "They're just like us?"

"I wouldn't say that. You can decide for yourself when you meet them."

On the basis of that promise, Delia stopped crying and waited until they arrived at the lake. Mr. Pearce didn't even pause to unload the car. Instead, he led Delia off immediately down the trail to the water. Intent on keeping up with his long, thumping strides, she scrambled blindly after and ran up against him when he stopped suddenly.

"Why, hello there," he said quietly, standing very still. "Are you the welcoming committee?"

5

Delia looked where he was looking, into the woods. For a moment she saw nothing but the thick trunks of pine and sharp morning shadows. Then came the movement, and she saw a boy stepping back from the trail. He was older than she, but distinctly different from her in more than age. He wore a plaid cotton shirt and blue jeans, which, like her own Saturday clothes, were faded and soft with washing. But his skin was the warm color of crusted loaves of well-baked bread, and his dark eyes, wide open in surprise, were set in a flat, oddly impassive face. His black hair hung in an even cut at ear level. Mr. Pearce held out his hand.

"I'm Fred Pearce, and this is my daughter Delia. We've just arrived at McPherson's Lodge." He continued speaking in his deep, soft voice. "It's Delia's first visit here. I'm taking her down to the water, to introduce her to the lake. Want to come?"

The boy hesitated. His stillness was so complete that he seemed to Delia to become invisible against the green shadows of the woods. When he stepped forward onto the path, she saw that he wore soft leather boots, fringed and beaded and tied with leather thongs. He stared at Mr. Pearce's hand, then slowly extended his own.

"You can't be Miss Rebecca's son," Delia's father said to him, looking at him closely. "Her grandson, perhaps?"

The boy nodded and looked at his hand, which seemed to have disappeared in Fred Pearce's grasp. "She is my grandmother," he said. "My name is Isaac."

"Glad to meet you, Isaac," Mr. Pearce said. He released the boy's hand, but steered him onto the path and began walking with him to the water. "How's she been, your grandmother? She's been running McPherson's kitchen for as long as I remember. You tell her I was asking for her."

Isaac nodded, and Mr. Pearce went on talking. Delia had followed behind them, focusing her attention first on the silent flutter of the fringe on Isaac's shoes, and then on the dappled shine of the sun on his black hair.

"What about the fishing?" her father was asking. "It's been a few years since I've fished the lake. I'll probably need some help finding out where they're biting. I suppose your dad's still guiding for Mr. McPherson's guests? No? I'm sorry to hear that. But construction work is good work, even though it keeps him away from home a lot. I'll bet you miss him. It won't be so bad in another year or two, when you're busy guiding your own parties on the lake."

The three of them came to the end of the trail, where the trees gave way to the black slate shore of the lake. Taking her hand, Delia's father walked with her down to the very edge of the water, where waves lapped irregularly on the shiny stone. He knelt beside her and trailed one hand in the cold lake, and together they looked out over the bay.

Gouged from the earth by glaciers, Lake of the Woods was a vast, irregular expanse of twisting shoreline, dotted with islands. Some of these thrust themselves up like medieval castles, gleaming white turrets of granite flagged with hemlock and spruce. Others lay supine in the lake, sheets of black slate, split and crevassed by millennia of freezing winters and thawing springs.

"Like it?" her father asked after a while.

Delia nodded. Here was a landscape worthy of her imagined new world. Satisfied, she turned to Isaac. "Can you skip stones?" she asked.

He could, she remembered, smiling out the car window. Gravely he had inspected the way she held the flat rocks in her small curved index finger and pitched them out over the smooth water. Then he'd skipped stones with her, that day and other days across the summers.

 **TWO**

"You're sure this place exists? Delia? Delia?" Jim's voice pulled her back into the sticky discomfort of the car. "You and your mother didn't just imagine it—some sort of mirage after all the hours of driving?"

"A driving delusion, Jim?"

"Really, Maggie." He groaned at her joke. "Why don't you just drive and leave the humor to Delia and me for a change?"

He spoke lightly, but Delia detected a flicker of annoyance in his tone. Maggie laughed a lot when the three of them were together, injecting a forced gaiety into all their conversations. That it might bother Jim as much as it did Delia had never before occurred to her.

"This trip makes me feel like one of Columbus's sailors," he said, turning back to Delia. "Are you sure, Captain, that we aren't about to sail off the edge of the world?"

Delia smiled. "It is a little like falling off the edge of the world, I guess, because it's so different from the rest of civilization. The lake is not the Loop, I can tell you that," she said, referring to the elevated commuter train that looped its way through downtown Chicago. "Maybe you won't like it."

"I wasn't always a middle-aged architect, Delia. In the dark ages of my youth I was known to wield a pretty mean fishing rod. The catfish in the river at home dug right in when they saw me coming."

"Catfish?" Delia wrinkled her nose in disgust. "There aren't any catfish in our lake, and it's a lot bigger than any river. You need a guide to find your way around, and charts. My father—" She stopped abruptly.

"Your father what?" Jim asked gently.

"Nothing. You should always carry a chart on the lake, that's all. Only fools get lost."

"Even your father lost his bearings sometimes, Delia," Maggie commented. "The people he considered fools were those who wouldn't take proper precautions, who weren't careful. He couldn't understand them."

"What sort of precautions?" Jim continued to address Delia, but it was her mother who answered.

"All the old standards that everybody knows about lakes and boats, but not everyone follows. Have the necessary number of life vests and cushions, don't overload the boat, have enough gas, carry a chart, let someone know where you're going and when you expect to be back. On a nice day, that lake is as peaceful as the local lily pond, but it can be treacherous."

Treacherous it was. To the uninitiated, the sparkling blue water gave a false appearance of safety. In moments its pastel calm could change to choppy gray. Clouds closed in on the lake as the storm gathered, and the wind beat white caps against the islands in wild, unpredictable patterns. Just before the storm broke, there was a hush like a huge, indrawn breath. Then, in a burst, came the sheets of rain and wind, the thunder and lightning. Delia had enjoyed the violence of those storms, standing beside her father on the porch of the cottage, damp but safe, brave as long as he was there. Now, like the storm itself, the fact of his absence broke over her. Delia shied from it, back to the present, to her mother and Jim.

"People do the craziest things when they go on vacation," Maggie was saying. "They lose all reason. We saw one family put five people in a boat that could only hold four. They had all the weight in the bow and a motor on the stern. When they started it up, the boat went straight down, just like a submarine. It went under, and they all sat there, sinking into the water with these big O's of surprise on their faces."

"At least they were near the shore," Jim said.

"Even so, it was almost a disaster. Not one of those people could swim, and only two of the children—the little ones—were wearing life vests. If it hadn't been for Delia, they would have drowned. She and one of the guides grabbed a couple of inner tubes from the dock and went in after them."

"It was Isaac, Mom, don't you remember?"

"I said it was one of the guides," Maggie answered. "Isaac was working for Mr. Mac that summer. But the point is that you saved some lives that day."

"It wasn't that big a thing. I'd been in swimming, anyway."

"Sounds to me like quick thinking," Jim said. "Good for you."

"It was Isaac's idea. If he hadn't been there, I'd probably have stood on the dock with everyone else and watched them sink."

"It doesn't matter whose idea it was," Maggie said. "Most of the youngsters wouldn't have been able to do what you did. And you were just a child."

"Twelve years old is not just a child, Mom. Besides, I'd already finished that course in lifesaving. I was supposed to know what to do."

"Still, you did it," Maggie insisted.

"And taking action is at least as important as knowing what action to take," Jim added.

"I suppose so," Delia agreed, hoping that would end the conversation. It was not the praise she objected to, but the deliberate effort Maggie made to brag about her, as though any good quality had to be exaggerated to compensate for her more numerous obnoxious traits. The smaller her success, the more Maggie went on about it, making Delia stiff and prickly with embarrassment.

"What about this other hero," Jim was asking, "this guide, Isaac? Who's he?"

"He comes from one of the local families who work at McPherson's resort," Maggie began.

"And he knows everything there is to know about the lake," Delia broke in, eager to talk about Isaac. "He's the best guide in the area. He's studying zoology and ecology."

"That's what he hoped to do, to work for the Canadian Wildlife Service," Maggie corrected. "He did have a way with animals. It seems to me every year he had a different collection of orphans, from chipmunks to skunks to wolves. And Delia was his number one assistant."

"I hope he's got something besides skunks and wolves this year," Jim exclaimed, "though I've heard that skunks make good pets."

"Isaac doesn't make pets of them," Delia said. "He wouldn't do that. He just takes care of them until they're grown and can fend for themselves, and then he lets them go. He says people shouldn't interfere with animals by trying to tame wild ones."

"He let those wolves go, Delia? Not around here, I hope. They were adorable puppies, but I'm not sure I'd think an adult wolf was cute."

"He was going to take them north when they were grown, Mom, when they'd learned to hunt, and let them go where they'd be safe from people."

"And vice versa," Jim said with a chuckle. "Even a partially grown wolf sounds dangerous to me."

"They weren't exactly running loose in the village,"

Delia said. "Practically nobody ever saw them. He brought them to show us, but mostly he kept them at his grandmother's."

"She has a little place on the outskirts of town. Really isolated," Maggie said. "We gave Miss Rebecca a lift home one afternoon, on our way to Kenora. The last five miles were nothing but a dirt track. I don't know how she manages."

"She hitchhikes," Delia announced. "All the Indians hitchhike. Isaac used to hitchhike to school."

"As you might have guessed," Maggie commented to Jim, "Delia spent a lot of time with Isaac that last summer."

"I spent a lot of time with him every summer. We're friends." Delia paused, swallowed and added, "Isaac and I and my father were friends."

"Friendly," Maggie emphasized. "We were friendly with all Mr. Mac's employees. Fred did try to help him, to give him some direction, keep him in school. I wonder how that all worked out."

"You can ask him."

"If we see him, Delia, but he's not likely to be around. That was three years ago."

"So?"

"You mustn't expect things to be the same this summer as they were then."

"Why not?"

"Things are different, that's all," Maggie said quietly. Jim reached over and rested his hand on the back of her neck. After a moment Maggie cleared her throat and continued. "Isaac should be finishing at the university, and Miss Rebecca's probably retired. They won't be at the lodge, neither she nor Isaac."

"But of course he'll be there," Delia insisted. "Where else would he go?"

"He could get a regular job, Delia, and have a home of his own. Just don't expect to find him at McPherson's. Now, what's this?" Maggie stepped on the brake and downshifted as the car slowed. Ahead of them, blocking the road in both directions, were two patrol cars. Warning flares were set at intervals along the roadside, and the lights atop the official cars shot red flashes into the bright daylight. "There must be an accident."

Delia sat forward, peering out the front windshield between Maggie and Jim. "There aren't any sirens or ambulances. It looks like the traffic is just piled up."

"Maybe there's something wrong with the road," Jim suggested. "A washout or a break in the pavement."

Nearing the patrol cars, they saw that white wooden barricades had been drawn across the highway, reducing it to single-lane traffic. On the far side, an officer was stopping and inspecting the cars heading south. As Maggie slowed up, a second uniformed officer stepped away from the barricade and held up a hand, signaling her to a full stop. Maggie rolled down her window as he approached.

"Afternoon, ma'am," he said, leaning over to look into the car. He nodded at Jim, then glanced into the backseat at Delia and the duffle bag of clothes. In that swift and casual look he noted the maps on Jim's lap, the freezer chest on the floor behind the seats, the pillows and nylon jackets on the rear window ledge. "Going on holiday, are you?" he asked, making it sound like a friendly, insignificant question.

"Why, yes, Constable," Maggie answered. "But we've already been cleared through customs. Is something wrong? I've got all our papers here somewhere." She reached behind the seat for her purse, snatching nervously for it as she spoke. "Do you need my driver's license? The customs agent said it didn't matter that my name is different on it and on my passport."

For a moment Delia thought she would go on to explain the family history, up to and including her marriage to Jim. But the officer was interrupting her, shaking his head.

"Nothing to worry about, ma'am. You're planning to stay at the lake?"

Maggie nodded.

"You have reservations? Someone's expecting you?"

"We have our own place," Delia spoke up. "But we park the car at McPherson's Lodge."

"You're familiar with the road, then?"

"Certainly," Maggie said. "We've been coming up here for years. Is there some trouble?"

"Just a local problem, ma'am. Have you seen any hitchhikers, picked up anyone?"

"No, we haven't seen anyone at all on the road, have we Jim?"

"I haven't." Jim bent forward to look at the officer. "We've noticed a lot of traffic, though. Are you fellows looking for something in particular?"

"At this point, sir, we're asking all visitors to the area to refrain from picking up strangers on the highway. We also recommend that you plan to reach your destination by nightfall, or check in at one of the motels along your route."

Jim glanced at Maggie, then turned back to the officer. "That sounds like a serious warning."

"No more than common sense, sir."

"Common sense doesn't require a roadblock," Jim said. "If you've got a bad situation developing here, we'd like to know about it."

The officer hesitated. "There was some trouble last night, sir, involving a couple of our men. We're watching the roads to make sure no suspects leave the area."

"What kind of trouble?"

"Nothing that should interfere with your vacation," the officer answered, and straightened up. "You can drive on, ma'am. Enjoy your stay on the lake."

"Thank you." Maggie rolled up the window, put the car in gear and drove slowly past the barricade. "What do you suppose that's all about?" she asked as she increased speed.

"I was just going to ask you the same thing." Jim turned and looked back at the cars stopped in the road. "They're after something, or someone."

"The border patrol was awfully careful checking the

car through customs, too," Maggie said. "I hope nothing's wrong."

"That's happened before," Delia reminded her. "They even examined my guitar case once. It all depends on which agent you get, you said."

Maggie frowned. "Customs used to be pretty much of a formality, with random checks to trip up people who were trying to avoid paying duty. But this is different. Jim's right. They're after something."

"There's contraband at any border," Jim said, "but you wouldn't think any smuggler worth his salt would try crossing at a checkpoint when he's got an unguarded lake at his disposal."

"It's not unguarded," Delia told him. "Wardens from the Wildlife Service patrol the lake. That's what Isaac wants to do, to help stop the poaching."

"For furs?" Jim looked over his shoulder at her. "I thought that kind of thing went out with French trappers and beaver hats."

"It's a way to make extra money. Most of the guides set trap lines in the winter."

"And they'd starve if they didn't," Maggie said. "They can't earn enough as guides during the summer to make it through the year, so they hunt and trap—and sometimes poach—to support their families."

"Isaac says there's no excuse for trapping or hunting out of season."

"I'm not saying it's right, Delia. But it's better than going hungry."

18

"They can always fish."

"When the lake's frozen over?" Maggie shivered. "I wouldn't want to sit out there for hours in the cold, watching out for the wolf packs that come down from the north. Besides, you'd feed the family a lot longer on a side of venison than on a fillet of pike."

"But it's wrong. And I think it's disgusting."

"You mean the killing?" Jim asked. "You kill fish, too."

"Don't remind me," Maggie cut in, deflecting their disagreement with a breathy chuckle. "Delia nearly had hysterics over the first fish she caught."

"It wasn't funny, Mom." With the clarity of a photograph, Delia recalled her father's expression of startled amazement as he stood at the cleaning table, the dead fish under his broad palm, the filleting knife already blooded, and watched her shriek. "You might have told me you were going to kill it."

"We just assumed you knew. Up here you eat fish, you don't catch them for pets. Even Isaac would agree to that."

"But not everyone's like Isaac," Jim commented. "At least, the other guides aren't, or there'd be no problems with poaching on the lake."

"You can be sure they aren't all like Isaac," Maggie said. "He is, to put it mildly, emphatic about ecology and the environment."

"It's just that he cares so much about the lake."

"I know, Delia, but sometimes his enthusiasms work against him. People stop listening to him."

"But he's right."

"That doesn't help his neighbors pay their grocery bills." Maggie sighed. "Things have changed so much since we first came up here. The roadblock, and those patrol cars—it's all familiar, but altered somehow. . . ."

"Is that what bothers you," Jim asked, "that it's different now?"

"If it were a different place entirely, it wouldn't matter so much. But it confuses me to look back, to try to balance what was with what is. It's much easier to start over." She paused. "I guess that wasn't very diplomatic of me, was it?"

"I didn't marry you for your diplomacy." Jim smiled at her. "We can still turn around, you know, cancel the trip."

At that suggestion Delia jerked forward. "We can't go back now," she objected. "We're almost there."

"That wouldn't necessarily make a difference," Maggie said, looking at her in the mirror. "But we aren't turning back. It'll be another hour before we arrive. Why don't you try to take a nap?"

"I'm not tired." She glanced from Maggie to Jim. "You weren't serious, were you? You wouldn't turn around, just because of that roadblock?"

"That's not all your mother's concerned about, Delia."

Maggie nodded. "It's the change. Things just aren't the same."

"And they shouldn't be. They can't be, Maggie," Jim said. "Don't forget that."

"But they can be," Delia whispered to herself, turning back to the window. Heat shimmered up from the road and rippled the deep green of the pine forest on each side of the road. "I'll make them the same."

THREE 🌿

Even before the car had come to a complete stop in the gravel parking lot of McPherson's Lodge, before Maggie could switch off the ignition, Delia had reached around, opened the car door and slipped out. The hot air tingled with the smell of pine, in contrast to the stale, dusty confines of the car, and the clear blue of the lake gleamed in the sunlight. From the pier at the bottom of the hill came the fresh scent of creosote and weathered wood, of motor oil and gasoline. Delia closed her eyes and breathed it in, then opened them again for a closer regard of the resort.

The Toyota was parked outside the main office—a large, wood-shingled building that also housed a small general store. The harsh winters, heavy rains and hot sun that had smoothed and weathered the shingles to an attractive, shiny gray brown had battered the green trim around the doorway and windows, leaving it faded and blistered. A bare bulb burned in the fixture above the door, forgotten in the glare of the sun, shining on the worn OFFICE sign. Across the front of the building was a screened porch that had provided a view of the lake. It was shaded now by young trees, with vines of honeysuckle thickening their trunks and hanging from their branches. The screens bellied out, like multifaceted fly eyes, winking at the dense growth. Through them Delia could see that since she had last been on the porch, its wicker chairs and couches had been replaced. Small pine tables and wooden chairs were clustered around the room. Set on the tables were citron candles and white plastic ashtrays slashed with red and black advertising. No one was on the porch, and there was no movement or sound from the office. Looking around, Delia realized that there were no other cars in the parking lot. Weeds and clumps of grass were growing up through the scattering of gravel, except in the area directly in front of the office door.

Delia turned toward the north side of the lot where a dirt road led into the woods to the cottages. There were no new buildings, only the familiar small frame structures set back under tall pines at seemingly haphazard but secluding distances from one another. Like the office, they were shingled and had green trim and roofs. They reminded Delia of a toy Lincoln-Log village with their bright peaked roofs and brown siding. Only the one nearest the parking lot appeared to be in use. Delia remembered it from summers past. For years her

23

parents had rented from Mr. Mac, even after Fred Pearce bought the island in Ghost Bay. Using McPherson's Lodge as a base, Delia and her parents had alternated between camping on the island and staying in the cottage on the mainland. They had done much of the construction of their island home themselves, using materials brought over the ice on trucks during the winter. Only their last summer at the lake, putting the finishing touches on their cottage, had been spent solely on the island.

Mr. Mac's cottages were clearly deserted. Only the one had door and windows open to the fresh air, while the shades were drawn in the others and the doors pulled to. Delia shrugged. Mr. Mac's rentals were none of her business. She and Maggie and Jim would load their things on the lodge's launch and pay Mr. Mac to taxi them across the bay to the island. She looked down at the pier, to see if the big boat was moored there.

Wooden steps set into the side of the hill led down to the rocky shore. Along the left side of the U-shaped pier was the double-berthed boathouse, and the gasoline pump at the open end. Tied in the protected center area were three aluminum rowboats. They rode low in the water, heavy with rain and lake water that had not been bailed out. Tossed aside behind the boathouse was a rotted red buoy. Near it on the shore, one of the round-bottomed, wooden Peterboro rowboats was drawn up, the bottom stove in. Delia's attention caught on it. There was an unmistakable mark of change.

24

Mr. Mac had sworn by the Peterboros that rode the lake storms like wide, heavy canoes, their glistening honey-colored wood slipping easily through rough water. Even here, aluminum was taking over.

Delia looked up then, out over the blue water. On the far side of the bay was her island, a wavering spot of land on the horizon, barely visible, but there, within reach.

"I'll find Mr. Mac," Delia said aloud to her mother. "We can load up the launch and be across before dark."

"No, wait." Maggie climbed stiffly out of the car. "That's pushing things a bit, Delia. We can't go out to the island today. It's already afternoon."

"But it's early. And it'll be light until almost ten."

"Delia, for once don't argue. We've been driving for two days and we're all tired." Arching her back, Maggie stretched the taut muscles of her neck and shoulders. "I could use a swim and a good night's sleep."

"Then we'll have to pack and unpack twice," Delia complained. "And why should we pay for one of Mr. Mac's cottages when we have a place of our own?"

Maggie dropped her arms and straightened her shoulders. "We've already decided to stay here tonight. I've made the reservations."

Delia opened her mouth to object futher, but Maggie held up her hand. "It's settled, Delia. I'm tired and don't want any more discussion about it. There'll be plenty of time to get out to the island later."

"But it's so close." Delia looked out across the bay.

During the weeks of preparation for the trip, she had not allowed herself to think beyond the details of the moment. Now, within sight of her destination, to wait one more hour was difficult, and to delay an entire day was unthinkable. She turned back to Maggie, prepared to demand or beg. But her mother did look tired. The bright sunlight deepened the lines around her eyes and mouth and flattened the planes of her face. Maggie's fair skin and hair, her delicate frame, gave an impression of fragility. Standing tensed beside the car, she seemed to Delia small and vulnerable.

"All right," Delia gave in. "But let's get an early start tomorrow. Maybe I can get Mr. Mac to start packing the launch this afternoon so we'll be ready first thing in the morning. Then we'll have all day to get settled. Mom? Mom, what's the matter?"

Maggie had closed her eyes and was rubbing her forehead, swaying slightly in the sunlight. "I told you, Delia, I'm tired. Let's just get our things out of the car and worry about the island tomorrow."

"But we've got all afternoon," Delia began.

"We'll discuss it tomorrow."

Jim had gotten out of the car and was standing with one hand on the door and one on the roof of the car. "Maggie, didn't you tell her?" he asked.

"Tell me what?" Delia looked from one to the other. "Mom? What didn't you tell me?"

But Maggie ignored her and turned to Jim. "It seemed pointless," she said. "It seemed pointless and premature.

I thought we'd go over and see it, and it would be clear even to Delia that we couldn't stay there."

"Stay where? What are you saying?" Delia grabbed her mother's arm, trying to regain her attention. "What do you mean, we can't stay there?"

"At the cottage, Delia," Jim answered her. "We think it's best to stay on the mainland."

"Stay here?" Delia swung around to her mother. Even to her own ears her voice sounded shrill, a childish whine. "But you promised."

"I promised we'd come back to the lake this summer."

"That's not what I meant and you know it. I want to stay on the island."

"I'm as eager to see it again as you are, Delia. But we don't know what shape the cottage is in, or the water pump or the generator. And we can't manage without water and electricity. We decided to stay here until we can check things out."

"And then we'll go?"

"We'll know better after we see it, don't you think, Jim?" Maggie turned to him again, her face tight and strained. "We did want to wait and see."

He frowned. "I don't think you should count on our staying on the island, Cordelia. We'll be spending some time there, of course. But there are just too many arrangements to make in too short a time."

"You do understand, Delia." Maggie reached out to touch Delia's cheek, to smooth her hair back from her heated face. "Surely you can understand that we don't

27

want to spend all of our vacation cleaning up a summer cottage."

Delia pulled away. "You don't have to do it. I'll clean it myself."

"Don't, Delia, please." Maggie's voice was soft and pleading. "Please don't be so upset. We are back at the lake. That's the important thing. We'll take a day or two to rest and unpack, then we'll go over and see what's what."

"A day or two?" Delia cried, her voice rising, cracking over tears of disappointment and anger. "We're almost there now." She waved a hand helplessly toward the horizon, toward the spot of land that was so unbearably close and yet so distant.

"We could have avoided this, Maggie," Jim said. "I thought you had explained."

"What could I explain?" Maggie replied, lifting her shoulders in a fragile shrug. "I didn't know, I don't know what the place is like. How could I explain?"

"Your plans, Mom, you could have told me what your plans were. Why didn't you just say that you'd reserved one of Mr. Mac's cottages?"

"I thought I mentioned it," Maggie said slowly. She looked down, studying the bed of crushed granite at her feet. Shadowed by the angle of her head and blue smudges of exhaustion, Maggie's eyes seemed too large for her face. "But I guess I didn't tell you. Maybe I thought it was obvious that we'd have to stay here, at least at first. But I never told you we'd stay on the island. I am sure of that."

"You never told me we wouldn't, either," Delia said, retreating from sympathy into anger. "You could have said something. Why do you always have to leave something out? At least I'd have been ready."

"I never dreamed it was this important to you, Delia. I thought being back at the lake would be enough. I just didn't realize. I didn't know."

"But you should have," Delia answered. Maggie's face appeared to her a pale blur of unhappy concern. She blinked the distorting tears away. "You just should have known. Never mind," she said, stepping back as Maggie reached out to her. "Forget it. Forget the whole thing. I'm going down to the lake." She turned away and half stumbled, half ran toward the path to the water.

"Delia, wait. Please."

"Let her go, Maggie," she heard Jim say as she left the glaring heat of the parking lot and stepped onto the shaded path. Pine needles crunched beneath her feet, and the woods closed around her in cool shadow. She began to run, pitching herself down the incline to the water away from Maggie and Jim, as though she could escape from them into a separate time and space. She ran through the spattering sunlight to the black slate of the lake shore, slipping on broken bits of scree as she neared the water's edge. There she knelt down on the cool, smooth stone and scooped the water up to her face, swallowing it in great gulps. It was shockingly cold, tingling against her hot cheeks. When her face was cool and her fingers numb with cold, she sat back on her heels and let her skin dry in the sun. The air was still, and only the small rustlings of birds broke the silence. Delia opened her eyes and looked down at the dark, glassy surface of the water. A pale and discontented reflection wavered back—her reflection. She brushed it away with a sweep of her hand.

"It isn't fair," she said aloud, watching the ripples of water catch and toss her image into meaningless patterns. "She had no right, not without telling me. But then, she never tells me anything."

The well-meaning neighbor women, so out of place in her mother's kitchen, had whispered to each other, "Does she know? Has Maggie told her yet?" Bringing their casseroles, meeting her school bus, holding the key to the empty house while Maggie waited at the hospital, they had known that Fred Pearce was dying. Cordelia had not. He had to have tests, Maggie said at first. Then came the treatments—a precaution according to Maggie—that reduced her father to bald thinness. He joked about his new image while Delia waited in a limbo of unconfirmed fears. Clinging to Maggie's silence, she ignored the whispers of the women. But those kitchen mutterings haunted her in the dark nights of her father's hospitalization. And still Maggie did not tell her, not until the end when, comatose and fleshless, Fred Pearce could no longer leave the hospital. Delia never saw him again.

"He wouldn't want you to remember him that way," Maggie had said, and Delia had nodded, frightened by the tired stillness of Maggie's own face.

"She should have told me," Delia said again, more quietly, smoothing the ripples of water with her palm as though she were wiping fog from a mirror. "Why couldn't she have told me?"

"Sometimes it isn't that easy."

Delia jerked around to see who was behind her. "Don't do that." She stood up to face Jim. "I didn't know anyone was there."

"I'm sorry. Are you all right?"

"I'm fine. Shouldn't I be?"

He stood looking at her, then took off his sunglasses. In the bright light reflecting off the water, his eyes were pale gray and troubled. "I'm not sure," he answered her. "That's why I followed you down here, to be sure you were all right. You seemed pretty upset."

"I got mad, that's all." Delia rubbed her hands dry on the seat of her pants.

"I can understand that. You're sure there's nothing else bothering you?"

"Like what?"

"Like being back here," Jim said, encompassing the horizon in the sweep of his hand. "Coming back here like this could be pretty upsetting for both you and your mother."

Delia met his eyes, her expression carefully blank. "I'm not upset," she repeated.

"Maybe you're not. But I want you to know that I'd understand if you were, and I want to help."

"You don't have to worry about me."

31

"Look, this would be hard for anyone. It's perfectly natural. Look at your mother."

Delia shrugged. "She says she's tired."

Jim stood quietly for a moment, looking at her. Then he bent down and picked up a piece of black slate that had sheared off from the slab where they stood. He flipped it over in the palm of his hand and ran his thumb over the thin, sharp edge. "I guess you're feeling pretty angry that she didn't let you in on our plans."

"Wouldn't you be?"

"Yes. I'd wonder why she didn't."

"You don't know her the way I do. She's always forgetting things," Delia said.

"You think she forgot?"

"She's been busy. When she's busy, she loses track of stuff."

"Sometimes people lose track of things they want to forget."

"Why would she want to forget the island?" Delia's voice rose. "She loves it."

"I'm sure she did love it. And would love it again if she were going there for the first time. But she's not. It's got a lot of memories for her, difficult memories." Jim looked down at the black stone in his hand. "Things are different now."

"For her, maybe. Not for me."

"That's what I'm trying to tell you, Delia—that they're different for you, too. They have to be. That's the way things are." He dropped the black stone onto the slate. "Nothing stays the same. It can't."

"Whose rule is that?" She faced him squarely, her feet planted slightly apart, her back rigid.

"Now, wait a minute," Jim said. "I didn't come down here to fight with you. I'm trying to help."

"I don't need your help."

Jim's eyes narrowed and his lips tightened. "All right," he said. "Then there's nothing else to talk about. Whenever you're ready, come up and we'll unload the car."

He turned away and moved quickly up the path to the resort office. Delia watched him go, staring into the woods at the arched branches and curling leaves of brush. They seemed to form a wall of colors and shadows, fencing her off from the mainland, leaving her trapped on the black spit of rock with the chill expanse of lake behind her. Delia shivered, suddenly afraid. She jammed her hands into the pockets of her denim shorts, pressing her cold palms against her own body's warmth. At the bottom of her pocket, her fingers touched and closed around the ridged bone handle of her father's clasp knife.

Imagining it once more in his large, strong hand, Delia held it out on her own palm, then snapped it open. Razor-sharp, the knife was a necessity on fishing trips. Fred Pearce used it for cutting everything from bait to impossibly tangled line. Like him, Delia kept the blade oiled and free of rust. It lay shining on her open palm like a magic talisman, and when she looked up, the path was clearly visible, the sunlight shining innocently in dappled patterns on the hillside.

Delia tried to shake off the residue of her fear. She'd

forgotten a lot of her father's lessons in woodsmanship if she could be spooked by an illusion of light and shade, especially with his knife securely in hand. Survivors don't panic, he'd taught her. She flipped the knife over on her palm. Reassured by its gleaming weight, she started up the path, hearing the rustle of the pine trees sighing in the afternoon breeze.

Delia stopped and listened. There was no breeze. Her entrance into the woods had silenced the birds and small forest animals. Yet she had heard the soft breath of movement, something heavier than the dropping of a leaf to the ground or a ripened berry from the stalks of wild raspberry. Turning slowly, the knife still open in her hand, she looked back at the shore, then to the right and left of the path. Coming full circle, she saw nothing, no one, in the cool shade. And yet she felt she was being watched.

"Who's there?"

There was no answer to her whispery but audible croak. If Jim had returned, if he had sent Maggie after her, they would have spoken up. Whoever or whatever it was remained silent. Looking back over her shoulder, Delia edged up the path, stepping backward onto a dry branch. It snapped in two with a resounding crack. Startled, Delia whirled around, tangling her feet in its broken pieces, and fell headlong up the path. The knife flew out of her hand into the brush. She lay stunned for a moment, then pushed herself up on all fours, shook her head to clear it and squinted into the underbrush.

The hair rose on the back of her neck as her eyes focused. Barely a foot from her was a figure, a man squatting in such complete stillness that he faded in and out of her vision like some sort of printed illusion of dots and colors.

Delia gasped and scrambled away from him, trying to back up the path. But she could gain no footing on the smooth bed of pine needles and slid helplessly toward him as his fist extended toward her. Unable to move out of his reach, she watched in horror as his hand stretched closer, opening. Then his fist turned palm up, the fingers spread not to grab her, but to offer the knife that lay open on his calloused palm. He remained motionless in the soft shadow, his black eyes meeting her wide, frightened ones. Delia stared at his face. His skin was a deep, weathered tan, and his hair hung in heavy thatches around his ears, as though it had been hacked off in chunks with a straight blade. His mouth was wide and thin beneath a straight, narrow nose, and his cheekbones were flat, triangular slabs. He was so thin that the tendons in his neck and forearms sprang out under his skin. Delia's hand shook as she reached out for the knife, half expecting him to clutch at her arm and drag her from the path. She snatched the knife back and, in that instant, recognized him.

"Isaac!"

"Go away. You don't belong here. Go home."

"Isaac, wait." Image tumbled upon image in Delia's mind, past and present, real and remembered, colliding chaotically. Although he wore the same heavy green-and-black plaid shirt and khaki pants, this Isaac was hardly the earnest boy she had known. Crouched on her hands and knees, she stared at him, confused and shaken by his transformation. "Isaac, it's me, Delia."

"Go away. It's not safe here." There was no glimmer of recognition in his tone or expression, no apparent interest in her. She might have been a total stranger, as unfamiliar to him as he now was to her. "You must leave."

"But we just got here. We're staying. The island . . . ."

"Forget the island," he broke in roughly. "Go home. Leave this place. You should never have come back."

"You do remember!" In spite of his forbidding appearance, Delia reached out to him. "What's wrong?"

"I told you. It's not safe." The harsh rasp in his voice softened, and his dark eyes looked back at her, revealing for that instant the friend he had been. "I've warned you," he said. "I owed you that much. Now, go away."

"Wait," Delia said as he stood up, uncoiling in one fluid motion. He nodded to her, but did not pause, and stepped back into the forest. Delia scrambled to her feet, ready to follow him. She thrust herself into the brush in the direction she thought he had gone, but she had lost sight of him. He had been taken in and shielded, only a few feet from the path, and had disappeared into the flickering light and shadow of the woods. She hesitated, uncertain where to turn, waiting for some sound or movement to direct her. She was standing quietly when the howling began, a thin wailing that sent cold shivers down her neck. It seemed to come from the edges of the lake itself, a high-pitched keening that fell on the deep silence of the evening and shattered it in reverberating echoes. Instinctively, Delia backed toward the path, moving away from the primitive baying, toward civilization. The sound continued, answered by its own echoes, and then by a thinner call that came from the woods beyond the cottages. The repeated howling and her own retreat from the woods covered all other sounds. Delia had reached the edge of the path before she saw the masked face and yellow eyes of a pale gray wolf. It stood stiffly on long, delicate legs, its head and tail held high, its ears erect, watching her. As she stumbled backward onto the trail, the wolf's ears flicked and twitched in response to the two distant howls. Clutching her knife, Delia regained her footing and stood still in the path, facing the animal. It watched her for another moment, then wheeled gracefully and trotted away, crunching gently through the brush.

FOUR 🌿

Delia bolted up the path to the top of the hill and turned down the dirt track toward the rental cottages. The Toyota was now parked under the pine trees, its hatchback open and partially unloaded, beside the open cabin Delia had noticed. Vaulting over the suitcases, Delia ran up the stairs, across the porch and into the cottage.

"Mom," she called, her anger with Maggie put aside for the moment. "You'll never guess what I just saw."

"Just a minute, Delia." Maggie was standing in the main room of the small cottage, her fingers lightly touching the back of an upholstered rocking chair. Opposite her was a tall, heavyset man holding a crowded key ring. Nothing in the room had been changed since Delia had seen it last—not the furniture arrangement, not the color of the walls, not the homespun curtains at the windows. It was shabbier somehow, clean but faded. Still, it might have been the same kerosene lamp, and the same worn oilcloth cover on the table. In the familiar surroundings, it was easy for Delia to imagine that her father had just stepped outside, leaving his favorite chair, the empty rocker, temporarily unoccupied. How many times in the years past had she gone off to find Isaac while her parents unpacked, and burst in upon them later with news of bears at the garbage dump or huge northern pike under the dock? With a strong sense of stepping back into those times, Delia stood in the cottage now and blurted out that she had seen a wolf. "And there must be more of them," she said. "Did you hear the howling?"

"Delia, wait just a minute. I'd like you to meet Mr. Mac's son. This is my daughter Cordelia, Mr. McPherson. My impatient daughter."

"How do you do?" Delia bobbed her head at the man, barely seeing him, and turned back to her mother. "It was right there in front of me, about two feet from the path."

"You must have left your manners at the border," Maggie said with her breathy, nervous chuckle. "Mr. McPherson and I are talking and you're interrupting."

"I'm sorry. But I never saw anything like it."

"You'll be seeing and hearing lots of things up here that you wouldn't come across in the city, little lady," the man said. "It was probably a dog, and loons you heard, not wolves howling."

"I've heard loons," Delia said, "and they don't sound like wolves."

McPherson looked at her through wire-framed, tinted

glasses that screened his expression. "Sure you aren't exaggerating just a bit?"

"I saw a wolf on the trail."

McPherson shook his head. His neck was short and thick, like a wrestler's, and his arms and shoulders were heavily muscled. His fingers were broad and stubby, like the unlit cigar he twirled. "It was probably a malamute," he said. "We've got some big dogs around here, and a few rough-looking mongrels come down from the Indian settlement."

"I'd know a dog if I saw one."

"Maybe, maybe not. It's not a good idea to be too positive, you know." He clamped the cigar in the corner of his mouth and tilted his head back so that his glasses caught the light. "Makes you look bad when you're wrong."

"I'm not wrong," Delia insisted. Behind her the screen door closed softly, and McPherson turned toward it, rotating his shoulders as though he could not move his head independently of them.

"It didn't sound like any animal I've ever heard," Jim said, carrying two more suitcases into the cottage. "But it wasn't human, either."

"There's nothing to be alarmed about," McPherson said quickly. The light glinted on the square panes of his glasses, giving his face a mechanical look. "Even if it was a wolf, it's miles away by now. That howling carries a long way, especially over the water."

"You needn't worry about us being frightened," Maggie said with a smile. "We've been coming up here for too many years to be scared off by the threat of wild animals."

McPherson swiveled to focus on her. "I didn't realize you folks were familiar with the area." He paused and rolled the cigar to the other side of his mouth. "You've stayed up here before?"

Maggie nodded. "In this very cabin. Delia's father started coming up here when he was a boy, half the age Delia is now. But the last time we were north was almost three years ago, when your father was still running the place alone."

"Three years?" McPherson folded his arms across his chest, and rocked back and forth on his heels. "That's a long time between vacations. I hope the old man didn't do anything to put you off. That's why I came in with him, to get things in order. He was letting too many details slip by him."

"It was nothing like that," Maggie said. "We've known your father for years."

"I don't recall his mentioning you. I never forget a name, but I don't remember any Marshall."

"It's Pearce," Delia said hoarsely. "The name's not Marshall, it's Pearce."

"Pearce?" McPherson stopped rocking and stared at Delia. "The ones who own Ghost Island?"

"That's right," Maggie said. "It's on the other side of the Traverse, at the mouth of Ghost Bay."

"I know where it is." McPherson stared at them, biting

down hard on his cigar, his eyes hidden behind the flat shine of his glasses. "I didn't expect you folks."

"Of course, you wouldn't have," Maggie said. "There's no way you could have made a connection between the names. Jim and I have been married less than a year, and the island is in Delia's name. When I made the cottage reservations I didn't bother to explain who we were. There didn't seem to be any need to go into it all—all the changes in our lives." She faltered, then went on. "They had nothing to do with our accommodations, after all. We just wanted a place where we could rest and relax. Nothing fancy. How much we all need a vacation, you can't imagine."

But Delia could. Whenever Maggie was nervous she talked too much and too fast, and her words were tumbling around her now. Sometimes it seemed to Delia that Maggie's voice would go faster and faster until it ran words together in a single, unintelligible blur that would spin itself out in a high, thin shriek. McPherson watched Maggie as though he were listening to something other than her words. He nodded as she finished.

"You just leave everything to me, Mrs. Marshall. If it's a vacation you want, that's what you'll get. We keep things real quiet here."

"So it seems." Maggie smiled rather apologetically. "It's almost as though it's deserted. We didn't expect to be your only guests."

"Things have been pretty slow. My father let the place go for a while. Takes time to build it back up.

But we're real glad to have you with us." The big man stretched his mouth into a smile. His teeth were small and even, stained to a yellowing ivory by his tobacco. He nodded. "You made the right decision in coming here, I can tell you. You sure don't want to be out on that island."

"Why not?" Delia demanded. Her stomach tightened into an icy knot. "What's the matter with it?"

"Nothing's exactly the matter," McPherson said. Behind his tinted glasses his eyes narrowed, appraising and dismissing Delia in one glance. "But there's a lot of work to be done. You can't just move into a place that's been vacant for three years."

"You mean it has to be cleaned. But there's nothing wrong with it."

"It's Delia's land and she's pretty eager to see it again," Jim said.

McPherson hesitated, then tried to smile at Delia. "We'll arrange a day trip anytime you want, little lady. But we wouldn't want you out there alone, the three of you. You're better off right here."

"But if it only needs a good cleaning, I can do it. There's no damage, is there?"

"I don't know that I'd call it damage, exactly. But you've got chimneys to clear, the pipes to flush out and the generator to start before you can even pump water. That's not my idea of rest and relaxation."

"No, but it wouldn't be impossible for us to stay there," Delia said.

43

"On your first vacation in three years?" He glanced at Maggie. "I wouldn't. You might enjoy roughing it, but think about your mom. Besides, that island's pretty isolated, little lady. There's no way off it without a boat. What shape's your equipment in after three years? Suppose your motor conks out, or the boat springs a leak? You're stuck. There's no telephone. You can't call for help if you need it."

"You're not suggesting that it's not safe, are you?" Maggie glanced at Jim, then back at McPherson.

"We were stopped by some troopers on the road," Jim said. "They gave us the impression that there's been some trouble on the lake."

"Then you've heard about the game wardens." McPherson took the cigar out of his mouth and looked down at it, considering the bitten end.

"We heard there'd been some difficulty."

"It was bound to happen sooner of later. If you ask me, Mr. Marshall, they were looking for trouble. But when one of their own gets killed, they don't like it."

"One of the game wardens was killed?" Maggie drew in her breath sharply.

"That's right. And the other's in the hospital with a fractured skull. I thought you'd heard."

Jim shook his head. "No, the constable only said there'd been some trouble. Are there any suspects?"

"They've got a warrant out. My father and I, we tried to warn them. You can't trust these local people. But the wardens wouldn't listen, and now one of them's dead."

The chill at the pit of Delia's stomach spread outward, up her spine and down into her fingers and toes. McPherson's announcement had filled the room, pressing into its corners and driving out any sense of holiday. Fear and worry tightened Maggie's lips and pulled sharp creases between her eyes. Jim stood very still watching McPherson.

"What exactly happened?" he asked.

"One of these young hotshot wardens took it into his head that there was some serious poaching going on. These youngsters—you put a badge on them and they think they can change the world. He'd heard about it from one of the guides, which was his first mistake. There's no sense listening to them." McPherson looked at his cigar. "Anyway, he started investigating, stirring things up."

"That didn't stop the poaching?"

"He got no proof. The constable, Davis his name is, and this Indian claimed there was a ring of poachers, but they had no evidence." McPherson hunched his shoulders, then rolled them back and straightened up. His bulk seemed to expand, dwarfing Jim and Maggie and Delia. "Davis and his partner must have stopped a boat last night. But it wasn't evidence they got. Davis was found on Government Docks this morning with his head bashed in, and his partner's body was in their patrol boat, adrift on the lake."

"At least he's still alive. He can tell who did it." Maggie shivered. "It isn't safe here until their attackers are arrested."

"That may be, Mrs. Marshall, but Davis isn't doing any talking right now. He's in a coma. There's some question about whether he'll even survive."

From where she stood to one side of McPherson, Delia could see his eyes flick behind his dark glasses from Maggie's face to Jim's. He wet his lips and put the cigar back in his mouth.

"I'm real sorry this had to come up on your first day at the lake," he said. "But you're in no danger. As long as you're staying here on the mainland, you're perfectly safe. And if you mind your own business when you're out fishing, you shouldn't have any trouble."

"But what about my island?" Delia asked again. "When can we go out?"

"Suppose you leave that up to your parents and me, little lady."

"There's more to it than Delia's wishes," Jim said. "I'd like to check out the property myself—see what condition it's in."

"Your father said he'd keep an eye on things for me." Maggie was frowning. "Has he said anything about that?"

"He'll be giving you a full report, Mrs. Marshall. In fact, he was going to contact you about renting or selling the place. Seemed a shame to let it go like that, year after year, with no one living there. You want to think about it—we could probably do business."

"We're not interested," Delia said.

"We don't have to discuss that right this minute,"

Maggie said quickly, shooing the subject away as if it were an annoying fly. "The main thing is to get unpacked and settled."

"And enjoy the vacation," McPherson added.

"We plan to." Jim held out his hand to McPherson, more in dismissal than friendship. "You'll tell your father we're here, won't you? I'd like to speak with him."

"I'll tell him," McPherson said. "You can count on that. He'll be real surprised to hear that you're back. I'll tell him, all right."

His hand tightened around Jim's, and the muscles bulged in his forearm. Jim ignored the pressure and managed to propel McPherson toward the door.

"If you need anything, you just call." McPherson stepped out onto the porch. "I'll be glad to set you up with a boat and a guide, whatever you want. Just let me know your plans."

"That's mighty obliging of you." The heavy edge of politeness in Jim's tone acknowledged McPherson's offers at the same time that it questioned them. The big man paused and looked down at Jim. His chest and shoulders filled the doorway of the porch. Jim stood relaxed, his hands hanging loosely at his sides, meeting McPherson's eyes. They faced each other in silence until McPherson dropped his head a fraction of an inch and turned aside. He pushed the door open and went down the steps, slamming the screen behind him.

"Just what was that all about?" Maggie asked.

"I'm not sure myself." Jim rubbed his hand and watched

the man stride away down the dirt path. "But I don't like his attitude. Why didn't he recognize you?"

"I've never met him before. Mr. Mac was always alone here, though I remember some mention of a wife and son in the States. I guess there are lots of women who wouldn't want to spend their lives up here."

"I suppose so." Jim turned around. "Are you sure you're going to be comfortable here? It's not exactly luxurious."

Delia and Maggie both looked around the small room. The cottage itself was like a rectangular box. The living area where they stood took up the front half of the building, with a kitchen and bathroom on the far end. The rear half was divided into two bedrooms by partitions that were the same height as the outside walls, leaving the inner roof of the cottage visible. The furniture was simple, but comfortable. There was an upholstered maple couch and chair, a low table on an oval rag rug, and a long pine trestle table and chairs in the dining area.

"It doesn't look particularly inviting," Maggie admitted. "But it is clean. It will do. When Miss Rebecca was here, there were always fresh flowers on the table for new guests. That alone made you feel welcome. You see, things do change, Delia."

"Miss Rebecca may be gone," Delia said, the words slipping out before she could stop them, "but I'll bet Isaac's not."

48   "No? Did you see him?"

"I saw someone on the trail, Mom, that I thought might be Isaac." Immediately Delia regretted mentioning their encounter. She tried to brush it off. "But it probably wasn't."

"I'd be surprised if he were here," Maggie said.

"It must have been one of the other guides," Delia agreed, realizing that if she wanted to stay at the lake, Isaac's strange behavior and warning, as well as his grim appearance, should not be shared with Maggie and Jim.

"I always thought the woods suited him better than people," Maggie said, sitting down at the table. "He was so shy. It took me five years to get him to say yes when I offered him a piece of cake. You could see he wanted it, but couldn't bring himself to say so. And he was always hungry. When he guided for us, we'd bring an entire shore lunch just for him. Not that it helped. He was still nothing but skin and bone."

"He was not." Delia struck out at the skeletal image her mother's words provoked. "You make him sound like some kind of freak. He was just tall and slender."

"Isaac never looked as though he got enough to eat. And he probably didn't, especially after his grandmother stopped working for Mr. Mac." Maggie paused and looked curiously at her daughter. "You don't have to defend his looks to me, Delia. I'm not criticizing him—I'm describing him. I didn't say he was ugly. I said he was thin."

"But he's normal. I mean, he wasn't thin because he was sick or anything."

49

"Of course not!" Maggie's hands fluttered up from the table to her face in sudden understanding. "No, Delia, I didn't mean that. I'm sorry. I didn't mean to remind you."

"You didn't remind me of anything." Delia turned to Jim and abruptly changed the subject. "I didn't like Mr. McPherson either. He seemed almost glad those game wardens got hurt."

"He didn't much like their not taking his advice, that's for sure. People like him try to push everybody around, as if their size gives weight to their ideas. I don't like bullies, and I don't like being pushed."

"Not all big men are like that."

"I didn't say they were, Delia." She and Jim faced each other from opposite sides of the rocker for another moment, then Jim shook his head, took a deep breath and bent to pick up the suitcases. "Suppose you get the rest of the things in from the car. I think we need to get settled."

For the next hour the three of them unpacked. Maggie put groceries away in the small aisle of a kitchen, while Delia and Jim hung up clothes in the two bedrooms. Delia liked arranging her things in neat stacks in the chest of drawers—the shorts and bathing suits for the hot afternoons, the long underwear and blue jeans for early mornings and evenings. Ordering her clothes in the peace and quiet of the familiar room was like ordering the future. After the long siege of change, the three years when the most commonplace routines of her life had been disrupted and distorted, the lake was an oasis of stability. Maggie hadn't rearranged the furniture here or cleared the cottage of all traces of her father. Her memory sharpened by her surroundings, Delia sensed his presence all around her. The images that came to mind here were like the photographs that Maggie had relegated to the attic, vivid portraits of the healthy man he had been. He belonged here. And in spite of his docksiders and denims, Jim did not. Everything about Jim was modern and streamlined, in direct and uncompromising contrast to the room around him. He was a guest here, a visitor. Here Delia could politely ignore him.

She straightened up, closing the last drawer with a solid thump, slid the duffle bag under the bed and went into the living room. Maggie hummed tunelessly in the kitchen, accompanied by the soft sounds of evening that drifted from the woods into the cottage. The glow of the setting sun seeped across the porch and into the living room, lighting the pine-paneled walls and floorboards to a golden sheen. It was a magical time, this first evening back at the lake, this moment of union between night and day. Delia closed her eyes and held her hands up to the westering light. It was a gesture both of petition and gratitude, a ceremony of thanks for this access to an unchanged past. As the sunlight slipped upward and touched her face, the rocking chair behind her creaked. Startled, Delia thought for an instant that her magical thinking had worked, that time had indeed buckled backward. Her eyes opened and she spun around, calling out across the years.

"Daddy?"

Her voice was hardly more than a whisper, but it silenced Maggie's song and froze Jim in the rocker. Delia stared at him, unable to account for his presence in the place that was uniquely her father's.

"No," she cried, brushing her hands across the empty space between them, as though she could erase him. "No, you aren't my father. I didn't mean you."

Then Maggie was beside her, cupping her cool hand over Delia's forehead. "Are you all right? I knew this was a mistake. We should never have come back here."

Delia blinked, and the room snapped from fuzzy gray back into solid lines of color. "I'm fine, Mom. It was just something about the light."

"More likely it's overexhaustion, or heat prostration." She felt Delia's arms and face. "You aren't clammy, but you're very pale. I think you'd better lie down."

"I don't want to lie down." Delia pulled back from her mother's touch. "I feel fine."

"People who feel fine don't hallucinate. A little rest won't hurt you."

"Isn't there a doctor anywhere around here?" Jim asked, sitting forward in the rocker. "Maybe we should have her checked."

"I'm not going to any doctor. I'm not sick." Delia looked at their pale, worried faces. "All right, then, I'll lie down. On the porch, though."

"Just for a little while, Delia, please. You don't want to ruin the vacation by getting sick." Maggie stroked her hand over Delia's cheek. "We'll see how you feel when you wake up."

"And if you need a doctor, you'll go to one," Jim said.

Delia ignored him. "I'll lie down, but I won't sleep. I'm not tired."

"At least try, Delia." Maggie followed her onto the porch, flouncing pillows for her and covering her with a cotton afghan from the couch. "I'll call you for dinner."

FIVE 🌿

Delia pulled the afghan up around her face, knitting her fingers through the openings of its design. It smelled of dust and mothballs, comforting in its pungent familiarity. She stretched out her legs and let her back muscles press into the hammocky softness of the couch. She could no longer picture her father in the rocking chair and perhaps would never again be able to find him there. Mentally she turned away, away from Maggie and Jim and from the blurred image of her father, and moved outside the room to the island, the lake itself, and Isaac.

Within the barely recognizable figure she'd met on the path was her summer companion, the small, solemn boy of those first vacations and the young man he became. He and Delia had both grown up over the years, changing during the long winters between their meetings. It was that image she recalled now, the Isaac

54

of three years ago, glimpsed on the shore of Cat Point in the cool, bleached morning light of their arrival at the lake on that last vacation.

Delia had burst from the car and run down immediately to the dock and boathouse, and then out to Cat Point to find Isaac. The trail curved through a thick stand of pines on the far side of the resort, down the middle of the narrow peninsula that formed one arm of McPherson's bay, ending in an open clearing. Delia pitched herself across the clearing and scrambled up the huge boulders that ringed the shoreline. Gaining the crest of the rock, she saw him below her, startled, his face tensed in surprise. She grinned and spread her arms wide in greeting.

"We're back," she crowed. Then, unbalanced by the rush of her forward motion, she teetered, swung her arms in a wild attempt to reverse her direction and tumbled down as Isaac's hand shot out to catch her. Crashing down on top of him broke her fall, and only his hard, sure grip kept her out of the lake.

"Are you all right?" he asked, helping her up. "Another six inches and you'd have been soaked."

"That's fine with me. You ready to go swimming?"

Delia watched the slow dawn of a smile on his face. He was so serious always, so intent on observing the smallest nuance of life around him, that he often seemed to Delia to be remote and distant. Only when she could coax his smile and see its warmth in his eyes was she totally confident of his friendship. He pushed his hat back on his head so that his heavy, thick hair fell tangled on his forehead and the sun caught on his face and sparkled in his eyes.

"Did you have to tumble out of the sky like that and scare me half to death?" he asked. "You probably frightened away every fish in the bay."

"Looks like you've got your limit, anyway." Delia peeked into the burlap bag that lay half submerged on the rocks beside them. "Is the walleye hole off Russell Island still good?"

He kept smiling, a gentle curving of the lips that made him look young and vulnerable. "You want a guide—you'll have to hire one."

Delia grinned back at him, looking up and trying to take in all the changes of one year in his face, his height. "You're taller," she said.

"So are you. You look different."

"It's my hair. I cut it." She shook her head and her dark brown curls bounced.

Isaac considered her in his slow, still way. Then he nodded. "Yes, it is different from your braids."

Delia waited, wanting him to say that she looked older, more grown up, prettier, listening for something comparable to what he said in her daydreams, something on which she could build new fantasies. He was as she remembered him, though taller by one or two inches and heavier through the shoulders and chest, still straight and finely chiseled, as though his features had each been formed by a single perfect stroke. His boy-ish slenderness had hardened into a young man's agility, and the rawness of his movements had smoothed into strength. Standing before him, observing and observed, Delia felt totally exposed. The bright sunlight was a beacon that illuminated and exaggerated all her faults. Her feet looked huge in her new gym shoes, monster appendages at the ends of her long, thin legs. There was a syrup stain from the breakfast pancakes on her blouse. Her hands dangled from her wrists, and her elbows jutted sharply out from her sides in skinny triangles. In that clear, unrelenting light, even the scattering of freck-les across her nose and cheeks was obvious. Delia was suddenly embarrassed, shy, distanced from Isaac by the physical changes in their familiar, reliable images.

"Are you going to leave those fish here to rot," she asked, poking at the burlap bag with her toe, "or are you going to clean them?"

"Are you going to help me?" He was teasing, knowing her aversion to the blood and slime of fish cleaning.

"If you'll teach me," she replied, jerking her chin up and meeting his eyes.

Isaac took a small fish from the bag, rapped it sharply at the base of the skull with the blunt edge of his knife to kill it, and stripped away the meat easily, quickly, as though he were removing a glove from a hand. He held out the knife. "Ready to try it?"

Delia knelt down beside him on the rocks. Gritting her teeth, she pulled a fish from the bag and laid it on the flat black rock where Isaac was working. It lay still for a moment, then flipped its tail and curved up and over, flopping down inches from the shallow water. Isaac's hard brown hand came down on top of it.

"If you let them get away, I won't eat tonight," he said, setting the fish back on the rock.

"Miss Rebecca won't let you starve."

"Miss Rebecca isn't paid by McPherson to cook for me," Isaac replied. He pointed at the fish. "Don't leave the poor thing to drown in the air. Kill it quickly."

Delia did as he told her and, following his directions, cleaned the fish. With Isaac's help she had two white, boneless fillets, somewhat more ragged than his, but respectable.

"How come you're not guiding a party today?" she asked, washing the fillets off in the lake while Isaac cleaned another fish. "You could be making lots of money and still have the fun of fishing."

"Some fun. Toting motors and stringing bait, untangling lines for greenhorn fishermen and keeping my ears and nose on my head while I do it. You call that fun?" He handed Delia two more fillets. She was surprised to see the deep creases of a frown around his mouth and the angry darkness of his eyes.

"I thought you enjoyed it—being a guide."

"For your father I do. But McPherson says I can't pick and choose who I'll guide for if I want to work for him. I'd rather depend on the lake for my next meal than be paid wages for guiding some of those people."

"Come on," Delia said. "It can't be that bad."

"You sound like McPherson." Isaac shoved the fish remains to one side. "He says I should be more humble, that I'd get along better. I don't see what that has to do with it. Half the people act as though I'm a non-person, and the other half. . . . Forget it. Never mind."

"The other half what?" Delia sat back on her heels and watched him as he filleted the fish. The knife flashed so quickly that the strips of meat seemed to jump like live things into his hands. "Are they all lousy fishermen?"

Isaac shook his head. "It's not that. I just wish they were all like your father. If it hadn't been for him, I wouldn't be going to school this fall. I wouldn't have known where to begin. He helped. He treats me like a person. But you wouldn't understand that."

"Thanks a lot!" Delia bristled.

Isaac passed her more fillets to wash off. "Sorry. Maybe that was unfair. It is different for you, though."

"What's different?"

Isaac held the knife still and looked at her. "What I mean is, most of the guests here treat the guides like servants at best. I suppose that's what I am, but I don't like being reminded of it. Besides, I'm a guide, not a handyman."

"If I were a guide, I bet I'd be treated the same way."

"I doubt it. You're not Indian. If you asked them to pick up their garbage, they wouldn't think you were out of line." He reached for another fish. "But that's only part of it. These people don't care about the lake. 59

If I didn't clean it up, they'd leave the campsites covered with junk. Film wrappers, cans and bottles—they'll throw them anywhere. I've seen loons strangled on beer tabs or starved because they got tangled up in plastic six-pack holders. But I'm not supposed to say anything."

"Not all tourists are like that."

"Not all, but enough." Isaac looked out across the bay to the open stretch of water. "I wish they'd all leave, before they kill and change everything."

Looking at the stern flatness of his face, the angry grip of his hand on the knife, Delia wondered if he included her in that wish.

"But they won't, you know," she said after a moment. "They won't leave."

"So I'd better learn to live with them?" His hands moved even faster over the fish. "Sometimes I think I ought to just go away, forget about school and find someplace where there are no tourists."

"Are you scared?" Delia asked.

He snapped around to face her. Only the speed of his movement gave away his anger. His face was tight, controlled. "Of what?"

"If I were going away to school, away from home for the first time, I'd be scared. I'd think of excuses not to go." Delia waited, a little frightened as always by the flatness of Isaac's expression. Then he shook his head, and his mouth loosened into a smile.

"I guess you're right. I am scared. If it weren't for your father and my grandmother, I'd be ready to forget the whole thing. I could just stay here, or go south and work with my dad. He could find me a place on one of his crews."

"And you'd spend your life being as homesick as he is. If you get your degree, you can live and work here."

"That's what my grandmother says. I just wish I could be sure it would help. Did you notice those trees as you came through the woods? There wasn't enough food for the deer last winter."

"You can't blame the tourists for that. Some of them probably even came up here to hunt deer. That would reduce the herd."

"Hunters kill trophy animals. It's natural predators like wolves that keep the herd strong. They kill the sick and old or injured, the ones that shouldn't reproduce."

"You can save the lecture for the hunters," Delia said. "What's happened to the wolves?"

"Farmers don't like them. They trap or poison them."

"Doesn't the Wildlife Service stop them?"

"That's the problem," Isaac said, even more seriously. "It's government policy to kill off predators. Then the other animals overproduce and die of disease or starvation."

"You think it's better to be killed by a wolf? Some choice."

"I'd take the wolf any day," Isaac said quietly. "Ever see one?"

"Only in the zoo."

"Want to see one up close?" Isaac took the last wall-

61

eye out of the bag and cracked it on the neck. "Real close?"

"Where?" Delia looked nervously over her shoulder.

"In the boat," Isaac said. "Be careful. They should be about ready for lunch."

"They? How many are there?" Delia craned her neck to see into the open boat that was pulled up on the shore of the point.

"See for yourself."

Delia edged over to the boat. In the bow was a worn, heavy blanket. As she watched, its folds fell back to reveal the prodding nose of one puppy, and the curved white tail of another. They made small yipping sounds as they stepped and tumbled over one another.

"I told you they'd be getting hungry." Isaac scooped one up and put it in Delia's arms. Its tummy was still baby-round through the soft but coarsening fur, but its eyes were a wide bright yellow, and its teeth were needle sharp on her thumb.

"Where did you get them?" Delia asked, rubbing her cheek in the pale gray fur. "They're beautiful."

"I traded for them with one of the men from the village. He said he found the puppies but he brought them across the lake in a fresh wolf skin."

"If he killed their mother, wouldn't he have killed the puppies, too?"

"I don't know. My people don't kill wolves unless we have to. And then it's a tribal custom to purify your weapon before you use it again. But Joshua doesn't

62

follow the old ways much. He could have done it and taken his chances with his rifle."

Isaac watched the wolf nuzzle on Delia's shoulder, then bent and picked up the other puppy. "Not that he'd have gotten much for that skin. It wasn't big enough to bring a good price."

"How do you know he didn't shoot the wolf for bounty, or for protection? Maybe it attacked him."

"There's no bounty on wolves anymore," Isaac answered. "But there's still a market for the skins. Collectors will pay big money for them."

"They pay people to kill a wolf? They hire someone to hunt it down for them?"

"Not just wolves," Isaac said. "Anything from bighorn sheep and moose to eagles."

"That's disgusting," Delia exclaimed.

"But profitable. And you know who got charged with the eagle killings? Indians. They used the feathers and talons for war bonnets and jewelry, not for their own ceremonies, but to sell. Collectors again. That's really disgusting."

He cradled the wolf puppy in his arms while he rearranged the blanket in the boat, then set the puppy down again. From under the seat he brought a knapsack.

"Normally I leave them at the farm," he explained to Delia. "But I was going to be out all day, and they still need to be fed. They were both whelped late into the spring."

"What are you going to do with them?"

"I'm not sure. I'm open to suggestions."

"I'll keep one. Please, Isaac, let me have one." The puppy wriggled higher on Delia's shoulder. She patted its head, running her hand back over the bristling whiskers of its muzzle, and over the floppy, silky ears. "Can't I keep it, please?"

"Your neighbors would love that." Isaac reached out and scratched the puppy's head. "It's a wolf, Delia, not a dog. It should run free."

"I could train it. It's like a dog, after all. Dogs did evolve from wolves," she argued. "Did you name them yet?"

"This is Rea." He rolled the puppy over on the blanket and rubbed her tummy. "And that noisy clown you're holding is Lobo."

"You aren't making pets of them, of course," Delia said, watching him.

"Naming them doesn't make them pets." He stood up and grinned self-consciously at Delia. "But raising them this way might. Not that I had any choice. They were so young when I got them that they had to be bottle-fed. Without my grandmother's husky, they'd have died. That dog treats them like her own pups."

"Then what are you going to do with them?" Delia asked again. "Can you keep them?"

Isaac shook his head. "They wouldn't be wolves, not the way they should be. I couldn't let them run loose. Even at my grandmother's they're a little too close to the village."

"But what will happen to them?"

"I'll take them out with the husky as they grow up. They'll learn to fend for themselves. And when they're old enough, I'll take them north and let them go. That won't be easy," he admitted.

"Suppose they get trapped or shot?"

"It's either that or a zoo." He took Lobo from Delia and set the pup back in the boat to be fed. "I'm not sure I did them any favor in trying to save them."

"Couldn't you protect them somehow?" Delia thought for a moment. "At home we always have pheasants in our yard during the hunting season, as though they know they're safe there. Couldn't you have a sanctuary for wolves?"

"Where? There's no place, not anymore."

"There must be something you can do. There have to be laws. You could get the law changed to protect them."

"Just like that I'm going to change the law." Isaac bent and scoured the blade of his knife with a handful of sand. "I wouldn't know how."

"That's no excuse. My father says you can do whatever you want—anyone can."

Isaac rinsed his knife and stood up, looking over the rocks toward the clearing. "Where is your father? I thought he'd be down here by now."

"He's probably lying down."

"Lying down? Your father?"

Delia turned quickly away from Isaac and the wolves.

She knelt at the water's edge and rinsed her hands, watching the pale glimmer of her skin, like the white meat of the fillets, waver in the clear water. "You asked where he was," she said, "and I told you."

"What's the matter with him?"

"Nothing's the matter with him," Delia answered, as if the crisp, easy lie could make it so. She had seen how weak her father had become, how the weight had sloughed from his body. Fred Pearce had been a big, meaty man with wide, heavy hands, who prided himself on his strength. But in the last six months he had shrunk as his body turned in upon itself, devoured by its rapacious disease. Delia stood up and shook the water from her hands. "He just needs a vacation, Mom says. He's tired, that's all. But there's nothing wrong, nothing really wrong."

She looked up then, meeting Isaac's eyes, challenging him to disagree with her. His dark gaze revealed nothing, but glittered back at her with the reflected lights and shadows of the lake water as it lapped on the black slate shore.

Delia opened her eyes to the dim light of the cottage porch. Isaac had known, she realized. He had known that summer that Fred Pearce was dying. Delia shook her head, shrinking away from the wasted image of her father as if it were a sticky cobweb. From the horror of that gaunt gray stranger she drew back, sealing him off in the dark catacombs of her mind behind a wall of other memories.

SIX

The sun was no longer shining into the cottage, but was low across the water. Deep, pearly shadows filled the porch. There was a light, hesitant tapping on the screen door. Delia sat up and swung her feet to the floor, but Maggie motioned her back, stepped past her and reached for the door.

"Why, hello, Mr. Mac," she greeted him. "How good to see you again."

Mr. Mac squinted through the mesh of the screen at them, looking carefully from Maggie to Delia and back to Maggie. With narrowed eyes he watched her open the door. Even then he held back, standing in the shadows outside the door.

"Come in," Maggie urged. "How are you? You're looking well."

That was polite, Delia thought, but hardly true. Mr. Mac looked older and thinner than she remembered him, and his face was more deeply creased, like an apple dried in the sun. The gray, drawn quality of his skin was not an illusion caused by the metallic screen. Even in the soft light of the porch, his face was pale and greasy with perspiration, though the evening was cool. He held his cap in front of him, turning it around and around in his hand.

"Miss Maggie," he said finally. "So it is you." His voice creaked and he cleared his throat. "You look just the same. Haven't changed a bit. Now, the girl there—I don't know if I'd have recognized her."

"Yes, she's grown some," Maggie said. "Come in."

But still Mr. Mac hesitated, looking closely at Delia. "Couldn't believe my ears when my son told me. I didn't expect to see you and the girl again." He rubbed the bridge of his nose between his thumb and forefinger, and blinked, but found no change in their identity. "But you're here, all right. You might have let me know you were coming."

"I just never thought—" Maggie let the sentence trail off. "Come inside. I'd like you to meet my husband."

Delia sat on the end of the daybed and watched Mr. Mac follow her mother into the living room. He shook hands with Jim and, at Maggie's urging, pulled up a chair and sat down with them at the trestle table. But for an instant his eyes flicked toward the door and the dirt path back to the office. He cleared his throat once more.

"Never thought to see you again," he repeated, squinting at Maggie. His surprise was almost comical.

He stared at her as though a closer, longer inspection would reveal her to be counterfeit. "Wouldn't have figured you to be coming north."

"It was Delia's idea," Maggie said. "And I didn't think at the time that it would hurt. Now I'm not so sure. But Delia was so eager to come back. I just wonder if it wasn't a mistake."

"Don't know about that," Mr. Mac said. "It would have been a big mistake to go out to that island, though. At least you had the good sense to come here."

"You mean, because of the work involved in opening the cottage?" Jim asked.

Mr. Mac's eyes shifted to Jim's face and then away. "There is that. It'd be a big job, no question about it. How many windows do you have on that place, Miss Maggie? Eight? Ten? All with solid shutters? Just getting them down would be a day's work. Better for you to stay right here."

"So your son seemed to think."

Again Mr. Mac looked sideways at Jim, then let his gaze slip down to the polished square of tabletop in front of him. "Then there's the machinery—the generator and the water pump. Can't tell what shape they're in."

"How does the place look? You have been over to check on it, haven't you?"

"It looks all right, Mr. Marshall." Mr. Mac rubbed at a spot on the wood with his calloused thumb. "But you can't tell much by looking. You wouldn't know about broken pipes, for instance, or any critters that might have got trapped inside. Ever see what squirrels can do inside a cottage? You wouldn't believe the damage."

"Your son said we could arrange a day trip to the island, just to take a look around."

"He did?" Mr. Mac's eyebrows squirmed up into the creases of his forehead. "He didn't mention it to me."

"When would it be convenient?" Jim pressed him. "Can we decide on a day?"

Mr. Mac took a deep breath. "That's not so easy. You see, the launch hasn't been working too well, and my son's boat is chartered for the next few days. Don't know why he told you you could go across," he added, half to himself.

"Things don't seem terribly busy here," Jim said. "You're still expecting guests for the week?"

"The charters aren't for folks staying here," Mr. Mac explained. "It's just a little business my son runs on the side."

"I see. We'd like to take a look at Delia's property," Jim said. It was clear even to Delia, listening from the porch, that Jim had given an order. The edge in his voice surprised her. "If you can't arrange that," he went on, "we'll charter a boat in Sioux Narrows."

"Now, there's no need for that, Mr. Marshall, no need at all. I'm sure we can work something out." The old man twisted in his chair. "When did you have in mind going?"

"As soon as possible," Delia broke in. She pushed herself up from the daybed and joined the adults at the table. "How about tomorrow?"

70

"That's pretty short notice. You've been away for a couple of years," Mr. Mac said. "It wouldn't hurt to wait a little longer. Another day or two won't make much difference."

"But it will," Delia objected.

"You seem rather reluctant to take us, Mr. Mac," Jim said. "We've already heard about the murder of the game warden, if that's what's troubling you. If you want to keep us off the lake until the killer is caught, say so. Just how dangerous is it to go across the bay with him on the loose?"

Mr. Mac rubbed his chin. The stubble of his beard scraped against the hardened palm of his hand. "This lake is dangerous enough that I don't make guarantees. A murderer on the loose doesn't do a lot for the odds."

"So these poachers are a threat," Maggie said. "It makes sense that if they've killed a game warden, they wouldn't hesitate to attack tourists."

"If it's poachers that did it, Miss Maggie."

"Who else could it have been?"

"There are some who have their reasons."

"But the constables said the wardens had stopped a boat."

"There's lots of reasons for stopping a boat, too. All this talk about poaching has just gotten out of hand, if you ask me. Bad for business. Young Davis got sold a bill of goods. What would professional hunters be doing up here?"

"Do you mean bounty hunters?" Jim asked.

Mr. Mac shook his head. "Trophy hunters, Mr. Marshall, men who kill to order. Davis says it's big business, a regular mail order agency for trophy-size skins, antlers, whatever. Not that he can prove it. It's all hearsay."

"But something must have started the rumors."

"I warned Davis no good would come of it. He was a fool, him and that partner of his, letting the locals cotton up to them like they did, listening to their complaints. That's what started it." Mr. Mac looked up at Maggie and Jim. His eyes slipped rapidly back and forth between them. "There was no evidence. Who'd believe an organized ring of poachers even existed up here, much less made the money Davis was talking about."

"There are collectors," Delia began. "They'll hire hunters."

Mr. Mac turned toward her. His face was shiny in the lamplight, and tinged by its yellow glow to a jaundiced pallor. "What do you know about it?" he said roughly. "There's no proof. For all the digging around they did, they couldn't find any proof. Davis was comparing it to the drug trade, with profits in the millions of dollars. They'd have found evidence of something like that, right?"

"Depends on how careful the poachers are, I guess," Jim said. "But you know a lot more about it than I do."

"I don't know anything about it," Mr. Mac said quickly, backing off. "Just what I hear around town." He looked down at his hands. His fingers jerked in an irregular drumming on the table, then stopped. After a moment he looked up again. "Poaching's a way of life up here. One of the locals needs a little extra cash, he's going to do a bit of trapping. And if it's not quite in season, so what? It gets him through the winter."

"It doesn't sound like the same kind of poaching."

"Maybe not, Mr. Marshall. The point is, Davis should never have listened to that Indian. I warned him not to get involved. You could say that he brought this on himself."

"That's a little harsh, isn't it? He was only doing his job."

"His job is to keep order around here, not to make friends with every Indian in the province who thinks he's been mistreated." Mr. Mac brought his hand down heavily on the table. "Look where it got him. His partner's dead and he would be, too, if he hadn't been found on Government Docks. I warned him. You can't trust an Indian. I know."

"Really, Mr. Mac," Maggie protested. "What about Miss Rebecca? She worked for you for years. And her grandson Isaac is a fine young man, decent and honest. Certainly you could trust him."

"Isaac?" Mr. Mac's voice crackled like dry leaves. "Who do you think I've been talking about, Miss Maggie? Those constables you saw weren't stopping traffic for the heck of it. They were looking for Isaac. There's a warrant out for his arrest."

"For murder?" Maggie and Delia spoke at once, their voices blending in disbelief.

"He's no good, I tell you. The quicker they get him behind bars, the better I'll feel."

"We can't be talking about the same person," Maggie   73

said. "Do you mean the Isaac who used to work for you? The one Fred encouraged to go to college?"

"That's the one." Mr. Mac nodded. "Went up to Winnipeg to school. The only thing he learned was how to hate decent people."

"But what happened to him? People don't change overnight."

"He didn't change. Now, don't misunderstand, Miss Maggie. I'm not speaking ill of the dead, or saying Fred Pearce meant any harm. He didn't know these people the way I do. But he didn't do that Isaac any favors fussing over him like that. Made him think he was special."

"He is special," Delia said.

"He's crazy," Mr. Mac said, ignoring her. "That's the best you could say about him. He's always been crazy, and it got worse. First it was the environment, and then he started reporting things to the Wildlife Service—traps set out of season, hunters using lights to stun their quarry, that kind of thing. He'd even call down his fishing parties if they didn't clean up the campsite the way he wanted it. And they were hiring him! Got so no tourists wanted to go out with him." He paused and licked his lips. "He had a real attitude problem. But he was a good guide, so I kept him on in spite of his talk. I even sent him over to check on your place a couple of times, just to keep him busy."

"Couldn't Miss Rebecca talk to him?" Maggie asked.

"He always listened to her."

Mr. Mac looked down at the table again. "She died two years ago," he said. "They had to get Isaac down from Winnipeg to bury her. Must say, I felt a little sorry for him then."

"I wish I'd known," Maggie said. "He was away at school?"

"And never went back," Mr. Mac said, with a contemptuous snort that might pass for a laugh. "If you ask me, it was a good excuse for him to quit. He didn't belong up there, and he knew it."

"There were the animals," Delia said. "Someone had to care for the animals."

"You mean that zoo of his?" Mr. Mac turned slowly and looked at her. The weathered wrinkles deepened around his eyes, and his mouth tightened into a thin line. "They didn't need any care. He had to be crazy, living with a bunch of wild animals like that. Even then I tried to give him work, for old Rebecca's sake. He was no fun to have around, I can tell you that. Sullen, ungrateful, always sneaking around. It was about that time he got so chummy with Davis."

"That's when the poaching started?" Jim asked.

"That's when Isaac started reporting it. It would have stopped right there if young Davis hadn't listened to him. Davis came around with a list of endangered species. A reminder, he said." Mr. Mac snorted again. "Up here, I told him, man is the endangered species. It's that hard to make a living. The last thing we need is a bunch of government agents coming in, ruining the tourist trade. But Davis wouldn't listen. He even worked with Isaac, trying to find evidence. Of course that stopped after the trouble."

Delia gripped her chair with both hands, almost afraid to ask. "What trouble? What happened?"

Mr. Mac hesitated, looking down at the table. Then, as if he'd made up his mind about something, he straightened and squared his shoulders. "I don't have to tell you about this lake. You know it's no place for amateurs. It can swallow people up without a trace."

"What's that got to do with Isaac?" Delia asked.

"I want you to understand that this was no simple accident involving a bunch of tourists. Every year we have people lost on the lake. But this was different. Understand?"

Delia nodded.

"Like I said, Isaac wasn't doing much guiding. I didn't like to send him out alone. Mostly I'd team him up with Joshua. But we were shorthanded one day, and I had a party of no-nonsense types who were out to fish. I gave them Isaac. They never came back."

Delia's breath caught in her lungs like arctic air. She looked at Maggie, but her mother and Jim were both too intent on Mr. Mac's story to notice her.

"There was a storm," he went on. "We sent out a search party as soon as we could. But we never found a trace of them."

"And Isaac came back?" Maggie asked.

"He turned up at the Narrows about a week later.

He said he'd gone ashore as soon as the weather turned and was setting up camp when the men panicked. They took the boat and left him stranded on the island, he said. Nobody believed him for a minute, but he stuck to it."

"No one found the boat, or bodies? Anything?"

"Not on this lake, Mr. Marshall. There's nothing to say those men weren't lost on the lake."

"But you don't think so."

Mr. Mac squinted across the table at Jim. The creases around his eyes deepened into hard lines of suspicion. "Those men weren't fools. They wouldn't panic. They knew better than to try their luck on strange water without a guide. And I'm not the only one who thought so."

"Isaac was arrested?" Delia asked.

"He was held for questioning, but without witnesses they couldn't charge him. Then they picked him up again a few days later on an anonymous tip. Someone claimed to have seen him alone in the boat. It didn't amount to anything, though, and finally they had to let him off. The constables watched him after that. He couldn't take two steps into town without getting pulled in, just to make sure he didn't start any trouble."

"But that isn't fair," Delia cried. "Suppose he hadn't done anything?"

"You'd think it was fair if you saw him skulking around town, or sitting up in the woods staring out at the lake with those black eyes of his. It'd give you nightmares for a week. He's capable of anything."

"You think he killed those men? But why? For their gear?" Jim's voice registered his disbelief. "And the warden, too?"

"Not for their gear," Mr. Mac said. "Because he didn't want them on the lake. He hates us all. He's crazy."

"He's not crazy," Delia said. "Isaac isn't like that. Those men left him—they must have. He wouldn't kill anybody."

"Tell that to the game warden," Mr. Mac said to her. "You don't know what Isaac would do. Remember that."

"Delia's known him for a long time," Jim said. "They were pretty good friends."

"That doesn't mean she can trust him. I knew him a long time, too, and I'm lucky I didn't get my throat slit." Mr. Mac spoke to Maggie and Jim. "That's why I had to let him go. Couldn't trust him. He was always snooping around down at the boathouse or out on Cat Point. I swear he followed me out on the lake sometimes. No telling what he was up to. And you never knew where he'd turn up. A couple of times I went out to check your place and found him there."

"On our island? What was he doing?"

"I don't know, Miss Maggie, but I told him I'd have him arrested if I caught him trespassing again. And he wanted no part of jail, not after that last time. But until the troopers pick him up, I don't recommend that you folks spend any time on the island alone."

"But if he didn't do anything . . ." Delia began.

"He's no good." Mr. Mac's voice rose, harsh and angry. "You take my advice and steer clear of him."

Maggie clasped her thin hands together, her rings clanking loosely around her fingers. "I'm so sorry to hear all of this, Mr. Mac. You're sure there couldn't be some mistake?"

"Isaac's mistake, maybe, for finally leaving a witness." The old man pulled out a handkerchief and mopped it over his face. But his skin still looked moist—pallid— and his hand trembled as he fumbled for his pocket. "That warden's hurt bad, but he ain't dead. I warned him, for all the good it did. And now I'm warning you."

"We appreciate that, Mr. Mac," Jim said. "We really do."

Mr. Mac pushed back from the table and stood up, pressing one hand into the small of his back as he straightened. "Not much of a welcome for you, I'm afraid, but we'll try to make it up to you. You just relax now and have a real nice vacation. Don't worry about that property."

"I don't see how we can avoid it," Maggie said. "I don't know what to do."

"Like I said, Miss Maggie, you might think some about selling. You know you're always welcome here. No need for you to hold on to that island if you don't want to. My son will be glad to take care of it for you, get you a good price. You just let me know."

"No," Delia said, pushing back her chair as she stood up. But Maggie spoke over her objection.

"Thank you, Mr. Mac. I'll keep that in mind."

The screen door closed gently behind him, and they heard Mr. Mac's footsteps receding down the dry dirt track. Delia remained standing at the end of the table. Maggie looked down at her clasped hands. The silence lengthened, as though each one needed a signal to speak. Finally Jim looked up.

"Feeling better?" he asked Delia.

"I'm fine," she answered, her eyes on Maggie. "You wouldn't sell the island, would you?"

"It's something to consider, Delia. That's all. Something I have to think about." Maggie stood up. "I don't know about you two, but I'm starved. Do you think we could make do with omelettes tonight? There's cheese and bacon, or ham, if you'd rather."

Jim reached over and touched her hand, covering it with his own. "Maggie, sit down. I think we need to talk about this."

"We can discuss it later, Jim."

"There's nothing to discuss," Delia said.

"There's the lake. And the island. And Isaac." Jim pushed Delia's chair out toward her. "Sit down, Delia. Tell us what you think."

Delia ignored the chair. "He's wrong about Isaac."

"Perhaps. We should have mentioned to Mr. Mac that you thought you saw Isaac."

"If he were in trouble with the police, he wouldn't hang around here. Besides, they're wrong. Isaac wouldn't hurt anyone or anything."

"Not three years ago he wouldn't," Jim said. "But can you be sure about today?"

80   Isaac's gaunt face, his eyes glittering above the hun-

ger-sharpened angle of his cheekbones, had shocked and frightened Delia. It was not only that his appearance had changed. That solemn inner calm was gone, replaced by something Delia could not name, a force that had driven him into the forest as a fugitive. But she would not say that to Jim.

"What's that got to do with my island?"

"Delia, try to understand that safety is a factor in any decision we make," Maggie said. "We can't just ignore what Mr. Mac said."

"You already decided not to stay on the island. Why should we sell it?"

"You heard what he said. Things have changed here. It's not the same place it was years ago. We have to consider that." She stumbled over the words and stopped.

"Why?"

"What your mother is trying to say, Delia, is that we may find that we can't use the island. If Mr. McPherson can get us a good price, we might be wise to sell it. We can still come here to vacation."

"You can't sell it. It's my island." Delia stood at the end of the polished table, gripping its edges with both hands, facing Maggie and Jim. The lamp above the table isolated the three of them in a cone of yellow light, sealing them off from the darkening room and the twilight outside.

"That's why we need to talk about it," Jim said. "We know how much it means to you."

"No, you don't," Delia said in the same carefully

conversational tone. "You don't know how much it means. It's my island. It's all I have left."

"How can you say that, Delia," Maggie broke in. "We have each other. And the island means a great deal to me, too."

"Then you wouldn't want to sell it."

"It's not that I want to. Try to understand, Delia. It's a complicated situation."

"It's my island," Delia repeated loudly.

"Is it yours if you can't go there?" Jim asked. "That's what your mother means, that it's complicated."

"If that's what she means, why don't you let her say it?" Delia leaned forward, bracing her hands on the smooth, polished surface of the wood. She wasn't shouting, but her voice burst out in oddly pitched chunks, like notes from an amateur bugler. "Why don't you just admit that you don't want to be here?"

"Cordelia!" Maggie's hand was cold, but her grip was strong as she shook Delia's arm. "Cordelia, stop it."

"It's true, isn't it?" Delia turned on her mother, jerking her arm free. "He doesn't want to be reminded that we were happy here. You don't, either. All you remember is sickness. You threw the rest away, and now you're trying to take it away from me."

Delia was shouting now, her words popping into the air like globules of hot fat, searing and burning whatever they touched. "You didn't even want him to get better. You said it was a relief. You weren't even sorry."

82   Maggie's hand shot out, stinging Delia on one cheek

with her fingertips, then rapping the other bluntly with her knuckles. Delia's head snapped back. The shock of the slap stunned and silenced her. For a moment there was no sound except the harsh rasping of breath that Delia at first did not recognize as her own. Then Jim's chair scraped backward, shoved aside as he came to his feet, while Maggie clung to the far end of the table, repeating softly, "Delia, oh, Delia."

"You can't sell it," Delia gasped between hard, seizing breaths. "It's my island."

SEVEN 🌿

By being very polite to one another, they managed to get through dinner. Sitting side by side at the brightly set table, bending over the cool gray stoneware plates, swallowing the custard-yellow omelettes, they might have been strangers dining on a cross-country train. They passed the salt and set their silverware down quietly and carefully, and did not let their eyes meet. It was as though she had committed some monumental social gaffe, Delia thought, like the new girl at school who had worn a velvet suit the first day, causing her to stand out from her more casually attired classmates in unrelenting embarrassment for seven hours. If she could have acknowledged it, passed it off as a sin of excitement and newness, laughing at the excess, she'd have been accepted immediately. But branded by her finery, she had shrunk from it, denying her difference and repelling any friendly advances.

Delia felt that same distance widening between her and Maggie and Jim as they each retreated from the blaze of her outburst. There was relief in their carefully civil behavior to one another, but no resolution. She had stripped away the pretense of family feeling, revealing a truth too raw to contemplate. Like amputees who still feel sensation in their lost limbs, Delia and Maggie and Jim continued to act out the severed roles of daughter, mother, father. But the charade took its toll. Maggie's hands trembled, clattering the silver ever so slightly as she ate. Jim's normally fluid motions became ragged, indecisive; he reached for his coffee mug and set it down again, unsipped. Delia chewed mechanically, counting between each swallow, forcing food down her dry throat with gulp after gulp of milk. At last they finished. Jim stood up.

"We'll do the dishes," he said to Delia. "You go on to bed."

She escaped to her room gladly. Under the heavy Hudson Bay blankets, she lay with her hands behind her head, staring up at the roof of the cabin. The pine planks of the unfinished interior were riddled with knotholes. By turning her head or squinting up at them, Delia could perceive different patterns, some like faces or animal shapes, others like the vaporous sweep of galaxies on the night sky. In all the years Delia had slept in this room, in this bed, those whorls of wood had remained constant, altered only by her imagination and the tilt of her head.

Delia had counted on that sameness, trusting in it as she had learned to trust in the permanence of the North Star. Sitting on the dock with her father during those first summers at the lake, she had listened to the story of Callisto, the Great Bear, honored by Zeus with a place in the heavens and fated by jealous Hera never to set below the horizon. Her father had pointed out the constellations, the Big and Little Dippers, and taught her to track the North Star from them. Undimmed by city lights and air pollution, the stars crowded the skies above the lake. Each year Delia added to the list of constellations she recognized, as Fred Pearce repeated the tales of the Pleiades, Orion, the Hyades, Cassiopeia, Andromeda and Perseus, Pegasus, and others. Sometimes he talked of black holes in the universe and burnt-out suns whose light blazed on toward earth. He told her of ships' navigators bringing down the moon with their sextants, setting a course across uncharted seas by the steadfast North Star. She wondered now why she had never asked him how long it would remain intact. Was its beam finite? Would it one day flicker out and leave earth's navigators steering on a ghostly beacon, extinguished centuries before their births?

Delia rolled over, away from that image. She hadn't asked because it had never occurred to her then to doubt. Once, on a particularly chill night of that last August, she and her father had crossed a field through winking clusters of fireflies. Downed by the cold, the insects had clung to blades of grass and flashed their meager signals.

"The world's turned upside down," he'd told her. "A universe upended."

Then it was only a clever illusion, making her feel that she was walking on the heavens. Now Delia knew the reality of that pretended chaos. With her father's death, both her parents had disappeared as surely as if they had dropped through a rift in the skin of the sky, leaving her groping for direction on a burnt-out star.

Even the memory of her father was corrupted by the grimness of his death. And she missed her mother, the Maggie who was not yet a widow, the mother with warm, firm hands and ready laughter. Only the lake, it seemed, retained its character, though its contours were altered by time and water level. The waters rose and covered landmark boulders, creating treacherous shallows; low-lying islands simply disappeared. Or the waters dropped in times of drought and new islands appeared, and isthmuses replaced narrow inlets. But within those variations the lake, like the knotholes in the ceiling, was the same. And Delia was determined to hold fast to that part of it she claimed as hers.

On the far side of the partition that divided her room from the rest of the cottage, the clank of dishwashing stopped and the light in the kitchen snapped out. After a few minutes Delia heard the murmur of voices from the living room, whispered but emphatic in disagreement. Abruptly the argument stopped. Her heels clicking briskly, Maggie left the room, crossed the porch and went outside. Jim followed her, the rubber soles of his shoes wheezing softly on the bare floors. For a long time it was quiet. Then Delia heard the creak of the screen door and Maggie's step, slow now, on the porch. She came back alone into the living room. There was a pause, a ragged intake of breath, then silence.

Delia lay stiff in the center of her bed. In spite of the blankets, her hands and feet were cold and her body felt brittle, as though her bones were strung too tightly together. She heard the rustle of movement outside her door and threw one arm over her face, feigning sleep. Her door eased open, and Maggie called her name. When Delia didn't answer, she crossed over to the bed. Delia felt her standing there, looking down, and lay very still, forcing herself to breathe slowly and regularly. Finally Maggie bent over and smoothed the blankets, touching her hand lightly on Delia's head. Her fingers were cold on Delia's scalp, like a flutter of snowflakes. For an instant Delia's resolve faltered. With one gesture, she could strike out her angry words and break down the wall that Maggie's slap had sealed between them. By reaching out, she could brook that haunted, unmeasured distance and be reunited with her mother in a solidly reasonable, intact world. But as her fingers trembled with movement in the dark and empty space, Maggie straightened up and turned away. In a moment she had gone.

Delia did not call her back. At first she lay stiffly in the bed, not thinking. And suddenly everything was clear—clear and incredibly simple. She sat up and pulled aside the curtain on the window over her bed. The moon had risen and the pines glimmered, marking the drop of land from the cottage down to the bay. There would be a single rippled streak of moonlight on the wet rocks and out across the lake, like a fluorescent compass needle on the black water, pointing to her island in Ghost Bay. Staring out into the dark woods, she could almost see her way, following in her mind's eye the shimmering path over the water to Ghost Island. After a long time she lay down, her decision made. Curled under the blankets she relaxed, warmed finally by the glow of her own body heat against the smooth, clean sheets.

When she opened her eyes again, it was early morning. Pale sunlight eased through the window, lighting a square patch on the end of her bed. Completely awake, Delia listened for other morning sounds, but the cottage was still. She slipped out of bed, made it up and dressed. Quietly she tiptoed out to the living room. The lamp above the rocker was still on, casting a sickly light into the room, in contrast to the bright morning. Delia reached over to switch it off and saw her mother, still dressed, asleep in the rocker. She was wrapped in the afghan, her head tilted awkwardly against the back of the chair. The door to the second bedroom was open. The bed was neatly made, and the room was unoccupied. Delia glanced out to the porch, but the daybed was unrumpled, the pillows tossed aside where she had left them. The bathroom door was open, and there was no sign of activity in the kitchen. Jim was not in the cottage. Delia tiptoed to the window. The car was still parked outside, and no one was in it. It certainly looked as though Jim had not returned at all to the cottage during the night. And just as certainly Maggie had been waiting for him, expecting him. Their argument must have been a serious one, Delia thought, for him to have gone off without telling Maggie. He couldn't have gone far. Then Delia nodded to herself. After leaving Maggie, Jim must have gone to the lodge where Mr. Mac would put him up. McPherson had plenty of unoccupied rooms.

Delia hesitated, reluctant to leave Maggie asleep alone in the empty cottage, but even more reluctant to confront her or Jim in the wake of their argument. After all, that was their problem. Let them settle it. Besides, Delia rationalized, picking up her Windbreaker, she had plans to make.

A mist still pink with sunrise hung over the lake, muffling the calls of awakening birds. Already there were people on the pier, fishermen who had chartered McPherson's boat and the Indians who would guide them. Their voices and the rattle of tackle were soft and hollow in the mist. Delia stood watching them from the top of the hill, beside the parking lot. The sleek white fiberglass boat was tied at the end of the pier near the gas pump, and one of the Indians was filling its tanks. Like the other guides, he was dressed in faded denims and sneakers, and wore a heavy wool shirt against the chill of the morning. Another guide was stooped over the bait locker, dipping minnows from the net tank into a metal minnow bucket. When he finished, he put the bucket in the back of the boat and began stowing rods and tackle boxes. Two other guides were lounging against the wall of the boathouse, apparently waiting for their parties to arrive. Two of the aluminum outboards were already packed with shore lunches in coolers, readied for smaller fishing parties. McPherson's charter business was thriving, Delia thought, even if the resort was not full. She glanced over at the office, half expecting him to emerge and shout orders at the men on the pier. But if he was supervising the preparations, he was doing it quietly and out of sight. Just the same, this was no place to attempt a surreptitious departure, even at dawn. She'd have to find another spot to launch a boat without being seen.

She looked off to her left, to the trail on the far side of the office. Cat Point was secluded, and deep enough to accommodate the draft of an outboard. Walking softly in her gym shoes, she crossed behind the main building and into the pine forest. As she neared the water, the trees thinned, the ground leveled, and she entered the clearing at the tip of the point. In the hollow of one of the flat rocks lay the ashes of a campfire. Delia stopped beside it and stretched out her hand to it. The embers were still warm. Delia glanced around, looking for other signs of campers, but the point seemed to be uninhabited. She started forward to climb over the boulders to the water's edge when a sudden angry voice exploded from beyond and below her. Delia jumped back into the shelter of the trees, startled.

"You bloody fool," the voice exclaimed, bouncing

back on itself in distorting echoes. "I should have known better than to trust you. You said you'd get rid of them. You said they'd never come back."

Delia could not hear the reply, low and mumbled.

"It's too late for that now," the first voice said. "They're here. Give me a hand."

Twigs snapped and pebbles clattered under large, booted feet. Whoever the men were, they were dragging something heavy along the shore, something that scraped on the sand and gravel. They splashed into the shallows, wheezing with their efforts. Then there was a silence, followed by a hollow thump and the almost simultaneous lapping of small waves against a rocking hull.

"That's one less to worry about, anyway." The voice rang hollow over the water. "You know what to do."

"Not me," the second man said, panting heavily. "I won't do it. I want no part of this."

"You don't have a choice."

"This wasn't part of the deal."

"Your stupidity wasn't part of the deal, either," the first man growled. "So I'd call us even."

"I won't do it."

"It's a little late to develop a conscience now." The first man laughed, a sound as chilling as the cracking of rotten ice underfoot. "You've left your share of carcasses for the vultures. You had no objections to this business then."

92   "That was different. Animals are different."

"Since when? Don't tell me you're afraid of ghosts."
Again the man laughed.

"You said there'd be no trouble."

"So I was wrong. Don't get any bright ideas about
backing out now. You'll do what I tell you to do."

"And if I don't?"

"You will," the first man threatened. There was a
pause, broken by the scraping sound of something shifting on the bottom of the boat. "We haven't got time
to stand around here and argue," he continued. "You
got us into this mess, you can get us out. I don't care
how you do it, as long as you do it."

"I'll need a little time, that's all. They'll leave. They
want no part of this place."

"I'll give you to the end of the week to get it settled.
But if they're not gone by Friday, we'll do it my way."

Delia stretched up on tiptoe, balancing against one
of the trees to see beyond the rocks. But she could
make out only the bows of two of the old round-
bottomed Peterboros and the backs of two men in wool
checkered shirts, their hats pulled low on their heads.
She dropped down, stirring the brush and twigs beneath
her feet.

"What was that? Did you hear that?"

"Quiet." The first man silenced the other. "Listen.
Did anyone see you come out here?"

"I headed toward the Narrows and circled back around
Russell Island."

"Maybe I'd better take a look."

93

Delia held her breath and pressed her back against the rough trunk of the tree. She could hear the wooden gunwales of the boats rub together as the man shifted his weight, standing up to climb ashore.

"Forget it. It was probably just a squirrel."

"A mighty big one," the first man replied. Again there was a pause. Delia could imagine the man looking over the rocks at the clearing, his eyes scanning it, spotting her tree, watching for some sign of a witness to his rendezvous. Delia shrank close to the tree, forcing her elbows against her ribs as the pungent bark dug into her back.

"Why don't I just go," the second man said. "It's getting late."

"Why not?" The other's voice was lower, but still audible. "What difference does it make if one more person knows we've been clearing our property of nuisance wildlife." He laughed again, a cold, splintered chuckle. "Let's get out of here."

Moments later the motors sputtered and caught, and the smell of gasoline drifted back from the water. The wake of the boats slapped heavily on the shore, then softened into the normal lapping of the breeze-driven waves. After a few minutes Delia edged around the pine and looked out over the bay. One of the boats was visible on the open water, planing upward as it increased in speed and curved gracefully away into the morning mists. There was no sign of the other one, though it could easily have made the distance to Russell

Island and be hidden now behind its bulk. Delia continued to watch, but the bay itself was calm and empty, and there was no sound of activity beyond the rocks of the point. She took a deep breath and relaxed. Her hands felt stiff, and she realized that she'd been clenching them. Her fingernails had left deep half-moon indentations in her palms. The combination of Mr. Mac's warnings and the ominous tone of the men's conversation had left her feeling jumpy and afraid. She shivered. She had braced herself so long against the tree that she was stiff and cold. She rubbed her hands together hard, trying to shake off the persistent chill. But the memory of that cold laughter reverberated through the clearing, robbing it of its warm calm.

Delia looked again at the rocks, trying to concentrate on planning her departure. It was obvious that she could conceal a boat off the point, pack it and leave the mainland without being seen. The men had at least made that clear. She had only to check the water side now, to make sure that the cover of Cat Point was not visible from the resort docks, and her escape route would be plotted. She shook her hands one last time and stamped her feet loudly to speed up her circulation and to rid herself of the clinging sense of apprehension, then stepped into the clearing.

A hard, sure grip closed on her arm, whipped it behind her and forced her wrist up between her shoulders, while another hand clamped over her mouth and nose. So quick and sudden was it that Delia noticed nothing until her arm was jerked back and up and the cool morning air was cut off. She tore at the hand, struggling to free herself from the suffocating grasp, unable to make more than a thin, mewling sound. She tried to kick, but her attacker lifted her off the ground so that she had no traction, no aim. Her right shoulder was strained to the limits of its socket. Sharp pain jolted from her wrist to her elbow and up into her back. Worse than the pain was the inability to breathe. The fresh air was like a tangible substance around her, touching her face and hair, tantalizingly unattainable.

Delia yanked her head from side to side, but the bony tips of her captor's fingers dug into her cheek and trapped her skull in the hollow of his shoulder. She scratched at his arm with fingers increasingly numbed and distant, slow to respond. The tops of the trees, the gulls on the lake, wheeled above her in slow motion, as if everything were slowing down. Black spots began to blink against the calm blue sky, expanding from small dots to blinding disks over her eyes, absorbing vision, pain, the will to struggle. She blinked aside the first spiral of darkness, and another crested over her, its velvety thickness shot with streaks of red and yellow.

Suddenly she was thrust violently forward and fell to her knees on the soft cushion of the clearing. Gulps of air burned into her lungs, and the ground seemed to pulse with her coughing gasps. Slowly, the world came into focus again. Between the braced supports of her hands Delia saw tiny bright green stars of moss. She lifted her head and saw the smooth boulders that ringed the point. Carefully, she gathered her feet under her, positioning herself like a sprinter at the starting line. But this was a race she was not yet able to run. Her ribs heaved, and her pulse thumped in her eardrums, in her throat, in her chest. Slowly she turned her head, looking over her shoulder to see who had released her from that strangling grip.

A solitary figure stood silhouetted against the pale morning sky, hands clenched in fists, breathing almost as hard as Delia. The thin, sharp angles of his shoulders showed under the heavy wool shirt he wore, its cuffs turned back over lean, muscled forearms. The hollows of his eyes and cheekbones were shadowed, giving him a skeletal look.

"Isaac?" Delia breathed, still poised to run. She blinked, then scrambled backward as two wolves, like wisps of cloud, slipped from between the rocks to Isaac's side.

"Don't move," he said. "They won't hurt you."

The wolves' ears twitched at the sound of his voice, but they remained beside him. After a moment, the smaller of the two lay down on the sun-warmed grass, its long and delicate legs stretched out toward Delia.

"Rea?" Delia asked. "And Lobo?"

Isaac ignored her question. "How long have you been here?" he demanded.

"There were two men. I thought they had left."

"I told you once this place was dangerous. Now are you convinced?"

Watching the wolves, Delia stood up, then sat down abruptly on the nearest boulder. Her legs were unsteady, as though the tendons had stretched too far and no longer held her bones in proper alignment. "But why? Who are they?"

"You didn't see anyone?"

Delia shook her head. "I heard them talking."

"Forget that. If anyone asks, you were alone on the point. You heard nothing."

"I suppose I was alone when someone nearly broke my arm and strangled me." Delia looked around the clearing. "Who was it?"

Isaac said nothing. He watched as she looked at him, then at the rocks that hid the shore, then at the wolves. They were alone on the point. With her left hand, Delia rubbed her right shoulder, rotating it gingerly, and let her mind skitter off down an unpleasantly logical pattern of thought. The sun was high enough to burn off the morning mists, but it brought no warmth. Delia tensed against the rock, clinging to it for strength.

"There was someone else here, wasn't there?" She knew there was not, but she wanted him to lie and wanted to believe his lie.

"I owed you one warning. I've given you two."

"You didn't have to be so rough." She blinked rapidly to control the tears of pain and fear that choked her throat and threatened to spill down her cheeks. "That hurt."

"I meant it to. Go away. Go home before you really get hurt."

"It's not that easy." Raising her voice to hide its trembling, Delia struggled to appear outraged rather than frightened. "What's the matter with you? I thought we were friends. I know you're in trouble. Is that why you want to get rid of me? Can't I help?"

"Help me? You want to help me?" He leaned toward her. Delia could see the muscles tighten along his jawbone. Poised against the pure blue of the horizon, his body was a taut, barely controlled threat. Instinctively, Delia pressed back against her rock, touching the throbbing marks his fingers had left on her cheek. However familiar he had once been, this Isaac was no one she knew. His hands, hooked now in tight fists, no longer had that fine and gentle touch that could calm the wildest animal or bird. His eyes were flat and hooded in his bony face, like glinting facets of onyx in a carved mask. Isaac had shed some portion of himself, or had had it stripped violently away, leaving an image that was only remotely recognizable.

"You want to help me?" His voice was a guttural croak, stiff and harsh with anger. "Then go away," he repeated. "Leave this place."

For another instant they stared at each other across the clearing. Rea had risen to her feet and stood beside Isaac, her ears dropping back against her skull. Lobo, too, was tensed, his ears and brow lowered, his yellow eyes mere slits in his masked face. The coarse fur of his ruff rose threateningly, so that he seemed to grow in bulk and weight. His whiskers trembled and his lips quivered with silent snarls. Sensing their threat, Isaac looked down at the wolves.

"Back, Lobo," he said. At the sound of his voice and

the quick, chopping gesture of his flat palm, the wolf eased back, then dropped on its haunches. Rea whined, flicked her ears forward and back, and then she, too, sat down. Isaac tilted his head up and closed his eyes to the morning sun. Slowly his fists uncurled and the muscles in his arms lengthened and relaxed. He took a deep breath and looked again at Delia.

"Delia," he said, and the timbre of his voice struck a lost note between them. "Delia, you don't belong here now. You should not have come back. Go away."

"But why?" Delia demanded, her voice reaching back urgently to his evocation of that other time. "What's happened?"

"It doesn't matter."

"It matters to me—the island matters."

Isaac shook his head. "No. Things are different now. Just go away. Don't try to go back there."

"They told you to say that. They must have." Delia stiffened against the rock. "They want to sell it, but I won't let them."

"Let it go, Delia." He straightened up and looked away from her across the open bay. "They'll take it, anyway, if they want it."

"No, it's mine."

"Yours?" He turned back to her. "Yours because you bought it? Because you paid hard cash for it? And who signed your receipt?"

"My father bought it," Delia began, stung by his words and confused by his anger. "I need to go back," she said. "I thought you'd understand that."

"Go away," he replied, in a cold and empty tone. His face had closed once more behind the brittle mask. "I've warned you now," he said again. "There won't be a third time."

"I won't give it up," Delia said, her own voice a cold hiss in the stillness of the clearing. "You can frighten me, but you can't make me leave, any of you."

She thrust herself forward, away from the rock, startling the wolves. They sprang to their feet and, in spite of Isaac's signal, moved restlessly around him, their ears laid back. Delia hesitated, then stepped out onto the path. Turning her back on Isaac and the wolves, she left the clearing and, without looking back, ran through the pine woods to the resort and the cottage.

EIGHT 🌿

Delia ran away from Isaac, away from his warnings and the angry grip of his thin hands, away from the wolves. She ran past the docks, quiet now in the clear, bright morning. The lake below her sparkled, reflecting the blue of the sky, serene and inviting. But Delia did not pause. She ran on to the cottage, down the dirt track and up the porch steps.

She caught the door before it slammed, but Maggie was no longer asleep in the rocker. She was not in the kitchen or bedroom. There was a note propped against the salt and pepper shakers on the table.

"Delia," it said, "I've gone to the office. Stay here and watch for Jim. Mom."

Delia stared at it, then crumpled it into a small pellet of anger and threw it as hard as she could across the room. It bounced off the wall and onto the floor, rolling back toward her. If Maggie was so concerned, why didn't she stay and wait for Jim herself? At the least, she could have waited until Delia came back. She might have shown some kind of interest in where her own daughter had been.

"He's all she cares about now," Delia said to the crumpled ball of paper. "I only complicate things around here. But not for long."

From under the daybed on the porch, where she had stowed it when they unpacked the gear from the car, Delia pulled the one-person inflatable boat. Intended as a toy, a float for her to swim from, it was sturdy enough to provide transportation. In it she could paddle from her island to adjacent ones for food or fuel. She would carry her knife and take the small fishing rod. From the tackle box she took a couple of lures, a spool of nylon line, some weights and bobbers, and a packet of hooks. As an afterthought, she also took the small hatchet.

In a waterproof canvas bag she packed her rain poncho and the provisions she would need until she was settled: a jar of peanut butter, crackers, some packets of dried milk, and a box of cereal, a box of dried apricots and a box of raisins. In the picnic basket she found her grandfather's metal mess kit, a clever little frying pan with a collapsible handle, which closed into a compact round pot about six inches across. Remembering the stories of victims of plane crashes who survived for months on tidbits of chocolate, she added a couple of thick English bars, the ones with the hazelnuts, and then tied the bag shut. From the picnic basket she also took a couple of boxes of paraffin-coated, waterproof matches, wrapped them in plastic sandwich bags and tucked them in the pocket of her Windbreaker. She would take only the clothes she wore, she decided, since the camping equipment and supplies were all she could comfortably carry. Satisfied that she had all she would need, Delia gathered it up and stowed it outside the cottage under the porch. She had just sat down inside when Maggie returned.

"Where's Jim?" she demanded, glancing around the living room. Her hair was tangled, loose ends shifting over her face as she moved. "He isn't back yet?"

"How should I know?" Delia asked. "I haven't seen him."

"I thought he'd be right back." Maggie was addressing Delia, but her eyes slipped over her daughter's face without any real contact. She kept glancing around the room as though she expected Jim to appear magically in a doorway, in a chair, behind her back. "Where would he have gone?"

"How should I know?" Delia repeated. "You're the one who had the fight with him."

The barb grazed past Maggie, who continued to look around the room. "It was hours ago," she went on, half to herself. "And it was only a disagreement."

"He didn't come back last night? That was some disagreement."

Maggie seemed not to hear. "I've checked everywhere."

"Maybe he went into town."

"But the car's here. Where could he go without the car?"

"Fishing. Maybe he went fishing."

"He wouldn't have gone out alone in a boat."

"Catfishing? Do you need a boat for that?"

"Don't you understand?" The pupils of Maggie's eyes were wide and black, swallowing up the blue. She stood stiffly in front of Delia, rigid with worry and lack of sleep. "Jim's gone."

"That's impossible," Delia said. But the depth of Maggie's anxiety had reached her. "Maybe he's at the lodge. He's probably still asleep."

Maggie shook her head. "I've spoken to Mr. McPherson. No one has seen him."

"He can't just disappear." Delia kept her voice steady. Maggie's stance frightened her. There was a falseness to her calm, like a deceiving glaze over cracked pottery, held together only to shatter at the first pressure. "Where did you see him last?"

"On the path," Maggie said in a low, careful voice.

"Then he can't have gone far," Delia said. "Unless he went out on the lake."

"He wouldn't have done that." Maggie stared at Delia with her wide, dark eyes. "We shouldn't have come back here. It was a mistake."

For you, maybe, but not for me. The words bubbled up in Delia's mind, and she bit them off unspoken. "What did McPherson say?" she asked instead.

Before Maggie could answer, they both heard the

scrape of footsteps at the door. Maggie lurched forward, then slumped against the lintel with a small sigh.

"Mrs. Marshall?" Young McPherson pushed open the screen door and stepped inside. "I've just checked the boathouse."

Maggie looked up at him.

"All our boats seem to be accounted for. Doesn't look like he took one."

"That's something, Mom. At least we know he's not on the water."

"Right." McPherson nodded approvingly at Delia. "Now, suppose you tell me exactly what happened. What time did you say your husband went out?"

"We went for a walk after dinner, about nine o'clock, I'd guess. And then I came back here alone." Maggie put her hand over her eyes. Her voice trembled and cracked. "It was so foolish. We were arguing, and I was upset. I thought he'd come right back after me."

"He wouldn't be the first one to lose his bearings around here, Mrs. Marshall. He probably got off the trail in the dark."

"I suppose so. I did have the flashlight with me. But it wasn't full dark. And it's morning now. He could see his way now."

"What do the books tell you to do when you're lost?" McPherson asked her. "They tell you to stay put. Your husband's got good sense. He's probably waiting to be found."

106   "He should have been back by now," Maggie insisted.

"Unless he was hurt, he'd have found the trail."

"Let's not jump to any conclusions. We'll get some men and search the area. If he's there, we'll find him."

"Where else would he be?" Maggie's lips looked bloodless, and white lines of tension creased the corners of her mouth.

"Just a figure of speech, Mrs. Marshall. Like I said, he's probably sitting under a tree waiting for us."

"I know something's happened to him." Again Maggie's composure broke, and she covered her face with her hands. "We should never have come back here," she repeated.

McPherson reached over and took her arm. His hand encircled it easily. Half lifting, half supporting her, he guided her over to the table and pulled out a chair.

"I think you'd better sit down," he said. "Why don't you just take it easy now, have a cup of tea and let me take care of things for you."

Maggie backed into the chair, gripping the table for balance. "This is all my fault. If I'd let you sell the place for me, none of this would have happened."

"Thinking like that won't do anyone any good. You know what they say about spilt milk, Mrs. Marshall. And as for selling the place, it's not too late. You want it on the market, I'll be glad to do what I can for you." He patted her shoulder and drew his lips back in a smile. "Of course, it has been vacant for three years. That's likely to affect the price."

"It's not for sale."

"I'd say that's up to your mother, little lady. I'll make a fair offer. You've got nothing to lose."

"It's my island, and it's not for sale." Delia squared her shoulders to face the big man. McPherson stopped smiling.

"Not for sale," he repeated, considering Delia. But he didn't challenge her further. "It's probably not a decision you should be making right now, anyway. There's plenty of time. And when you're ready, you can let me know."

"What are you going to do?" Delia asked.

"First thing is to get that tea. Your mother could use a strong cup. How about putting the kettle on," he said to Delia.

"I'm all right." Maggie straightened up and ran her fingers through her tangled hair. She took a deep breath. "But what about Jim? You'll organize a search party, Mr. McPherson?"

"You leave it to me. I'll get some guides together and we'll check the area."

Maggie nodded slowly. "There's just one thing," she began. "I wonder if we shouldn't notify the police." She paused and waited until her voice had steadied. "There's already been some violence on the lake."

"There's no sense in looking for trouble, Mrs. Marshall," McPherson said quickly. He dropped his huge hand down on her shoulder. "Let's not make this more serious than it is. You have a little argument, your husband goes out for a walk to let off steam and gets lost in the woods. No reason to think it's anything more than that."

"I suppose not. Still, I think the authorities should know."

"There's time for that. My men know these woods."

"Isn't there something I can do? I hate just sitting and waiting."

"Best thing for you is to get some rest. You let me do the worrying for now. What happened to that tea?" he asked Delia.

Reluctantly, Delia left the living room, went into the kitchen and filled the kettle, placed it on the gas burner and lighted the flame. By the time she got back to the living room, McPherson had gone. Maggie looked up at her.

"Have you had breakfast?" she asked.

Delia shook her head. "Not yet."

"Let's eat something, then, before we get to work."

"Work? I thought you were tired."

Maggie nodded. "I am. But I want to be ready when Jim gets back. It will be easier to wait if I'm doing something."

"Ready? Ready for what?"

"We're leaving, Delia. As soon as he gets back, we're packing the car and leaving here."

"But Mom. . . ."

"I said it was a mistake, and it was. That's no reason to live with it. The sooner we put all this behind us, the better off we'll be." She paused and added quietly, 109

"It's not that I don't want to remember the good times, Delia. It's that they are part of a past I can't retrieve. I can't go back. I can't stay here."

Delia stared at the cup in her hand, watching the tea darken from pale gold to tan to dark brown. The silence stretched between her and Maggie until she set the cup down.

"I'm sorry," Maggie said.

By noon the packing was done, and by two o'clock, when they had had no word from McPherson, Maggie could wait no longer. She stopped her pacing back and forth across the living room, looked at the clock for the fifth time in as many minutes, then picked up her shoulder bag.

"I'm going up to the office," she said. "You can come if you want. It'll save time in the long run, if we have to go up to Kenora."

Delia did not ask why they would have to drive the fifty miles north to the town of Kenora. It was the location of the nearest hospital. In silence, she followed her mother down the dirt track to the office. The resort was quiet. No boats were at the pier, and the woods around the cottages were still except for the scampering of chipmunks among the dried leaves. But parked in front of the main building was a white car with the insignia of the Royal Canadian Mounted Police. Maggie began to walk faster, her strides lengthening until she was running the last few yards to the office. She yanked open the door.

"You found him?" she asked, startling McPherson. He was leaning on the counter over a chart of the lake, talking to the policeman from the squad car. "Don't be afraid to tell me. I want to know."

"There's nothing to tell, Mrs. Marshall. My boys are still out there."

"But surely by now they've searched this area. What about the lake?"

"You said he wouldn't be on the water. You have to give us some time."

"Somebody missing?" the constable asked. He looked from the chart to Maggie, then to McPherson. "What's going on?"

"You haven't told him?" Maggie didn't wait for the answer. "My husband's missing. He's been gone since last night."

"It's nothing, Allyn," McPherson said quickly. "Your men have got enough to keep them busy right now. I can handle this."

"Maybe you can't," Maggie objected. "We were right here on the property. If Jim had only gotten lost, you'd have found him by now."

McPherson leaned back down on the counter, hunching his bulk confidentially toward the officer. "They had a little argument, and Mrs. Marshall is upset. I'm sure her husband will turn up."

"This is not just another domestic quarrel." Maggie faced the constable. The rigid fear, the limp dismay that Delia had seen in her mother that morning were gone, replaced by calm purpose. "We did have an ar-

111

gument, but that wouldn't have kept Jim away this long. Something's happened to him."

"Didn't I see you folks on the road yesterday?" The constable looked closely at Maggie and Delia. "You just arrived at the lake?"

"That's right. And after talking with you and the McPhersons I was ready to pack up and leave again. But Jim thought we hadn't given ourselves enough time. If only I hadn't argued with him about it, he'd be here right now."

"Where exactly did you see him last, Mrs. Marshall?"

"Right there on the path." Maggie motioned vaguely to the area outside the office. "That's why I'm sure something's wrong. You haven't arrested anyone for the game warden's murder, have you?"

The constable shook his head. "No, ma'am, we haven't. And we have precious few leads. We're still looking for Isaac Smith."

"I'm afraid Jim's had an accident." Maggie paused, closed her eyes for a moment and then went on. "Or worse, that he's run into that murderer. There's no other explanation. He couldn't possibly have gotten lost for this long between here and Cat Point."

"Cat Point?" Delia was barely aware that she'd said the words. All too clearly she recalled Isaac's suffocating grip, the anger that transformed him. He had released her, he said, because he owed her that much. But he owed Jim nothing. With his tattered clothing and ragged hair, his eyes dark with caution, Isaac was like a hunted animal, dangerous because it has nothing left but its life to lose. Like the wolves he had adopted, he would attack if cornered. Delia's loyalty to what he had been stopped her from blurting out that suspicion, but her realization showed in her face and Maggie saw it.

"Delia, what's the matter? What is it?"

"You didn't tell me you went to Cat Point."

"Didn't I? What difference does it make?" Maggie was frowning at her, trying to read Delia's expression and reach the truth behind it. "What about Cat Point? Were you there? You saw something?"

Delia nodded, choking on the words that would betray Isaac's presence. But Maggie made the leap for her.

"Isaac?" she asked, reaching out to steady herself on the counter. "Delia, did you see Isaac? And you saw him yesterday, too, didn't you? It was he."

McPherson caught Delia by the arm, spinning her around. "You saw him and didn't report it? Where was he?"

Delia looked blankly at him. Maggie answered for her.

"On the path to the water, where she saw the wolves, remember?"

"Those blasted wolves!" McPherson exclaimed. "I should have realized he was around." Still gripping her arm, he gave Delia a shake that rattled her teeth. "And he was there today, on Cat Point?"

"Delia, how could you?" Maggie's voice rose. "Why didn't you tell me?"

"I didn't think it mattered." Delia spoke finally, finding her voice.

"But you knew Isaac was wanted by the police."

"Isaac wouldn't hurt anyone." But even Delia heard the doubt that colored her voice like a bruise.

"You don't know that. And you couldn't have known it yesterday when you lied about seeing him. Even after you heard what Mr. Mac said about Isaac, you kept quiet. Why, Cordelia?" Maggie paused, then rushed on, not really interested in a response. "You put our lives in jeopardy, and for what? For your own selfish reasons. And now Jim may be—" Maggie stopped, breathing hard as though she'd been running. "Is your island really as important as that?"

Delia could only shake her head, denying everything—the true and the false. Outside the small office, the wide reaches of the lake quivered in the sunlight. Delia wanted nothing more than to escape into that space, away from the darkly threatening atmosphere that was closing around her. But distances seemed to be collapsing, crumbling in on her like buildings detonated by a wrecking crew. The warped perspective of her reduced horizons revealed Ghost Island, her island, as a vanishing point that slipped farther away with each effort to reach it.

"It's not my fault. You can't blame me for it." Delia lashed out at her mother, battling the fear that rose inside her. "I didn't fight with him."

114   Color came suddenly into Maggie's face. She reached

out and, seeing Delia stiffen, dropped her hand. "Of course not," she said. Her voice shook with her effort to control it. "I'm not blaming you, Delia. We're all at fault. It was a mistake to come here. And we'll leave as soon as we find Jim."

"If the Indian was on Cat Point this morning," Allyn said, "we've got a place to start. We can fan out from there. Do me a favor, Mac, and call the Narrows. Tell them I need every available man they can find. I'll put a bulletin on the car radio."

"You don't really think he'd still be hanging around here, do you?" McPherson asked. "My guess is he's long gone."

"Guesses don't make arrests." Allyn started toward the door. "Just get the station for me."

"Wait." Maggie stopped him. "What about my husband?"

"If he's not on the mainland, Mrs. Marshall, we'll extend the search to the lake. Better get your boats gassed up, Mac. We may need them."

"You won't find Marshall on the lake," McPherson objected. "He didn't have a boat. What's the sense?"

Constable Allyn looked at Maggie before he answered. "If we don't find him, we'll have to assume he's with the Indian."

"That's pretty unlikely, Allyn." McPherson ignored the constable's attempt not to alarm Maggie further. "He wouldn't want any extra baggage to slow him down. Forget the lake."

"He may think a hostage will be useful. We'll search the lake if we have to." Allyn swung around and went out the door.

"We'll have constables and game wardens shoulder to shoulder around here," McPherson grumbled as he picked up the phone.

"But that's what we want," Maggie said. "Isn't it?"

McPherson nodded as he dialed. "Sure. That's what we want."

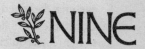

NINE

The search continued into the evening. Sitting in the office, Delia watched Maggie deal out hand after hand of solitaire. She played erratically, missing and ignoring moves but shuffling carefully between each game. She held the cards like time itself in her hands, counting out the hours of Jim's absence in spades and hearts, diamonds and clubs. Delia looked at magazines, flipping the pages but watching Maggie.

Jim had to come back. Delia tried to tell herself that Maggie's concern was excessive, that Jim would walk unharmed into the office any second. And she knew that when he did, all chance of her returning to Ghost Island was gone forever. Maggie would never retract her decision to leave the lake and sell the island, no matter how unfair or unnecessary it was. And it was unfair, Delia thought, her anger with Maggie swelling. If Maggie had not made an issue of the problems on the lake, there'd have been no argument and Jim would have been with them, sitting safely in McPherson's cottage.

But suppose Jim did not come back. The thought pierced Delia's anger again and again. She and Maggie were bonded together by guilt over Jim's disappearance, but could give each other no comfort. Delia saw the degree of her fault mirrored in Maggie's eyes. As the evening darkened into night, the tension built. When Constable Allyn finally entered the office, Delia jumped to her feet as quickly as Maggie, hoping for some news, any news that would end the waiting.

"Mrs. Marshall, I'm sorry," he said quietly. "There's no trace of your husband. I've called the search off for tonight. Until daylight there's nothing else we can do."

"And then?" Maggie stood with cards scattered around her, twisting her hands.

"Then we'll spread out on the lake. There's nothing more you can do, ma'am. Why don't you try to get some sleep."

Maggie and Delia returned to the cottage together, yet they were isolated from one another, separated by a gulf of guilt and uncertainty. It was easier, Delia thought in the silence of her room, not to witness directly Maggie's anxiety or her muffled recriminations. She knew she could not spend another day waiting, watching her mother's hands tremble over the cards. She had to take action, and there was only one action

to take. Dressing carefully, Delia climbed into bed. She

lay tensed and overheated beneath the heavy blankets, keeping them pulled up to her chin, in case Maggie looked in on her.

The edge of the rising full moon caught in the corner of Delia's window, casting a sliver of bleached light across the foot of her bed and into the shadowed, silent living room. Delia watched it widen and blend with the yellow lamplight from Maggie's bedroom. Then Maggie's lamp went out. After a long time, the rustle and creak of her movements stopped, her restlessness overcome by exhaustion. In the stillness Delia could hear her deep, even breathing. Slipping out of bed, Delia pulled on another heavy sweater and tied her Windbreaker by the sleeves around her neck. She tiptoed out to the table. It would be easier to leave without explanation. But the habit of years of leaving notes was hard to break, and Delia did not want to add her own disappearance to Maggie's worry over Jim. She took a sheet of notebook paper and, after a moment, began to write.

Mom: I can't sit by any longer and do nothing, knowing you blame me for our having come to the lake. Don't worry. I can take care of myself.

She hesitated, then signed it, "Love, Delia."

She propped the note carefully against the kerosene lamp, took a flashlight from the shelf beside the door and crept quietly out of the cottage. In the light from the moon, she gathered her gear from under the porch, hooking the loops of the canvas bag over her shoulder, and picked her way along the trail toward the boat-house. There were no lights from the lodge, or from Mr. Mac's apartment in the rear of the building.

In the moonlight, the resort and its surroundings took on an unfamiliar quality. The cool white light absorbed the colors of the woods and rocks, and reduced everything to shades of gray and black. Gleaming with dew, the ferns and mosses beside the path to the boathouse looked like transplants from some exotic landscape, with Delia the alien among them. The howl of an animal echoed over the water from a distance, a long and lonely baying that raised the hair on Delia's neck and slowed her steps as she looked behind her, remembering the wolves. The trees and bushes seemed to reach out toward her, their intricate thickness a reminder of her own vulnerable aloneness. In spite of her resolve, she shivered nervously and her heart thudded in her chest, crowding her lungs and shortening her breath. Jagged sweeps of shadow cut across the moonlit path like furred beasts. At every unexpected brush of leaves, her breath caught in her throat. But she forced herself to go on, easing down the hill to the boathouse.

Not unexpectedly the door was locked, but the water side had been left open. Years ago Delia had learned to climb out on the foundation rocks and swing from the eaves around the corner of the boathouse onto the catwalk inside. Readjusting her baggage so that it hung evenly on her back, she made her way across the wet rocks. She took a deep breath and jumped blindly, scrabbling for a grip on the roof, knowing that she had only one chance. A loud splash into the lake tonight would, quite likely, bring McPherson and his rifle. Somehow she caught and held on long enough to swing around and into the boathouse, dropping with an echoing thud onto the boards. It was an eerie place in the shimmering moonlight. The launch rocked gently at its mooring, the guttural lappings at its hull sounding like accents of a foreign language. Beside it, white and sleek, was young McPherson's speedboat.

Delia waited until her eyes adjusted to the shadows, peering into the far corners of the building to make sure she was alone. Nothing moved, and, except for the creaking of the launch, there was no sound but her own breathing. Carefully, Delia moved to the side of the big boat and slid aboard.

The launch was an old inboard with brass fittings, refurbished and maintained by Mr. Mac. It was long and low and rather boxy, dependable rather than fast, stable during the worst of storms, and roomy In the front, under the deck, was a small space for life jackets, heavy towing line and blankets. Delia opened the brass hitch and flashed her light inside. With some reorganization there would be enough room for her. She tucked the canvas bag to one side near the low-hung doors and arranged a nest for herself among the life jackets and blankets. Her raft, flattened and folded into its can-

121

vas carrying bag, made a waterproof barrier between Delia's gear and the water that sloshed in the bottom of the boat. The telescoping paddle and her fishing rod she laid along the side of the launch, their tips well forward into the bow. It was a tight squeeze, but Delia was able to pull the doors to, if she kept her legs curled up under her chin.

Settled at last, Delia was impatient for the dawn. Her plan was simple. When Constable Allyn extended the search for Jim to the lake, he would use all available boats, including Mr. Mac's launch. The range and size of the launch made it a logical choice for crossing the bay to search the more distant islands in the vicinity of Ghost Island. When the launch had gone far enough to rule out returning Delia to the resort, she could reveal her presence and offer to help in the search for her stepfather. It would be easy to slip away once Jim was found and, using the rubber raft, make her way to Ghost Island. The property was hers, after all, and she had a right to make claim to it. The worst that could happen was that Maggie and Jim would come after her. But at least she'd have seen her island again, and made her point.

She tried not to consider that Jim might not be found. If he were lost here on her lake, during the vacation she'd demanded, Delia knew she could not face Maggie and the stony endurance of her loss. Maggie probably wouldn't even care then that Delia was gone. Could she be a runaway, she wondered, if no one wanted her back? She wriggled against the life jackets, pushing aside the cold metal of a buckle. In either case, there was no place now for her but Ghost Island. She turned uneasily in the cramped quarters, waiting for dawn.

Suddenly the launch dipped to starboard, then balanced itself. Startled, Delia jerked forward, cracking her head on the low ceiling of the storage space. She peered through the narrow slit between the hatch doors, but the faint gray light of the boathouse was only slightly brighter than the blackness of her cubbyhole and revealed nothing. She strained to hear some sound, some movement from the cockpit. For a while there was nothing, as though someone were listening just as intently for some sound from her. Then she felt the launch shift again and heard the faint squeak of the rubber bumpers on the gunwales. In a moment there was the padding of bare feet above her head as someone crept across the bow to free the bowline. And then the boat began to move, slipping slowly and silently forward in the black water.

Staring through the crack in the doors, Delia watched the light change and brighten as the launch slipped out of the boathouse and continued to move in total darkness and quiet across the smooth water, powered by an unseen force. Of one thing Delia was certain. Mr. Mac was not that force. Whoever was taking the boat out did not want to be caught at it. Delia tried to shift her position to get a better view through the crack, 123 fearful of any sound that might give her away. She waited, huddled stiffly at the doors.

The boat glided on through the water until it was well away from the boathouse. Delia heard the scrape of wood on wood as her unknown companion stowed his paddle. Pressing her eye to the opening in the hatch, Delia saw a figure bending over the stern. As he straightened, his head, with its long, uneven clumps of hair, and his shoulders, hung with ill-fitting clothes, came into silhouette against the brightening sky. It was Isaac.

There followed a series of thumps and metallic chunks before the motor coughed, sputtered and caught. For Delia, lying close to the wooden hull, the noise was deafening, exaggerated by the earlier silence. After a moment, the din subsided as Isaac adjusted the choke and put the motor in gear. The boat trembled forward, easing its way into the open water. Then Isaac thrust the throttle forward and the launch leaped up, tossing Delia back against the doors. The bow rose, then leveled off as they picked up speed, beating in measured jolts over the choppy waves of the open bay. With each bounce her head bumped the deck above her, and her body was jounced against the ribs of the boat. Bracing her feet against one side and her shoulders against the other, Delia managed to stay in one position long enough to pull the life jackets around her as cushions. She had no idea which way they were going, only that they were moving fast across the night-black lake.

She could hear nothing now but the motor. She dared not switch on her flashlight, though she thought she could make out the twinkle of the white running light on the stern of the boat through the small gap still open in the hatchway doors. Finally, overwhelmed by the steady throb of the motor, Delia drifted into a kind of trance defined by the noise and darkness of her hiding place.

At last the pitch of the motor changed and dropped, then cut out entirely. The boat glided silently forward, touching shore with a soft thud. Again Delia heard the footsteps on the deck above her head, and then the splash of an anchor. She waited, watching the slim crease of light between the doors, holding her breath against the possibility that Isaac would inspect the hatch and discover her hiding there. But he remained in the cockpit, tinkering with the controls. At last Delia felt the boat tilt heavily and heard Isaac slip into the shallow water and wade to shore. Then it was quiet.

Slipping her knife from her pocket, Delia ran the blade up the slit between the hatch doors, unhitching the brass catch. Carefully she pushed open one side. The moon had set, and the sky had begun to lighten with the dawn. A few birds fluttered and called from the trees. Her cramped legs moved awkwardly as Delia crawled out, dragging the canvas bag and her inflatable boat behind her. They had moored in a tiny harbor formed by two slabs of rock that dropped from a high cliff into a crescent shape about thirty feet across. There

125

was a small sandy beach below the cliff face, with a narrow slice to the right that led back to the interior of the island. In the channel below the island was a small rocky slab where gulls perched. Delia stared at the shoreline, at the familiar rock formations. Incredibly, Isaac had brought her directly, immediately, to the place she had least expected to see—Ghost Island, her island.

After the months of preparation, the disappointment of Maggie's decision not to stay on the island, the shock of Jim's disappearance, Delia could not believe that her island was so clearly there before her. She fought the desire to spring openly from the launch to the shore, knowing she had to remain hidden from Isaac at least until she had determined his reasons for coming here. Peering over the bow of the launch, she surveyed the shoreline carefully, recalling its particular contours and the distinctive formation of its rocks. It was a small bit of land, only a few acres, but it had good drainage and a natural harbor, and it was sheltered by the arms of Ghost Bay from the storms that blew both north and south across the lake. Isaac had brought them through the channel into the bay, and circled around to the rear of the island. The dock and boathouse were at the far end, where the gradual slope of rocks provided the best foundation for them. The level of the lake was lower than Delia remembered. The black mark of high water stood out on the white cliff face four feet above the lapping waves. Other than that, she noticed no change.

Delia gathered her things quickly. Since he had made no effort to conceal the launch, Isaac must plan to return to it soon. If she could reach the shore without his seeing her, he'd never know she had stowed away, and she could watch him from the green depths of the island. She scanned the shore one last time, then clambered over the bow of the launch and jumped ashore.

Images of other arrivals on the island flashed in vivid projection in her memory as her feet crunched on the beach. The sand was coarse under her palms and still cold with dew and dawn. As she crouched there, the pebbles scraped and cut her hands, reminding her that this was reality, yet the present seemed to shear away. The lake slapped hollowly against the rocks and the tall pines rustled, suggesting the forgotten notes of her father's voice. Delia straightened up and moved forward, thrusting toward the center of the island as though she could wrap herself in it, gather it around her like the warm wool of a blanket. She started up the faint path, forgetting Isaac, the wolves, Maggie and Jim, everything but the sweet moment of return.

The moment was short-lived. Cutting across her consciousness, as palpable as the switch of a pine branch across her path, came the sudden high-pitched howl of a wolf. It broke from the interior of the island as though from the rocks themselves, shattering the stillness. The skin prickled on the back of Delia's neck as the howl was repeated, then answered, the two cries blending in a chorus that silenced all other sounds on the island. Stopped in midstep, Delia glanced around.

To her left along the shore the trees grew close to the water, overhanging deep, rocky pools, forming green tunnels of birch and linden. Quickly Delia ducked under their low branches and picked her way beneath their cover until she came to a mossy bank between two projecting boulders.

Making sure that the rocks concealed her from above and the arching branches hid her from the water, Delia set down her canvas bag, her boat and paddle. She could do little to defend herself from Isaac and his wolves if they attacked her, but she could be prepared to escape from them. She had the advantage of knowing they shared the island with her, while they did not. Surprise could be useful. With her back to the water, Delia settled herself to inflate the small boat, her eyes on the forest above her. Through the screen of pale leaves it looked unremarkable enough. Except for the baying of the wolves, which would have been a normal part of a deeper wilderness, the island was commonplace, exactly what an island at dawn should be. Carefully she unrolled the raft and blew it up, resting at intervals. By the time she had finished, the wolves' howls had diminished and soon ceased. Slowly the bird songs resumed, and the buzzing of insects.

With her means of escape secure, Delia relaxed and realized she was hungry. She unpacked her provisions and set out breakfast. Scooping some water from the lake, she mixed it with the dried milk, poured it over the cereal in her mess kit and ate. Hunger, her father had always said, was food's best seasoning. In comparison with waffles or pancakes and syrup, or fresh eggs and bacon cooked over an open wood fire, her breakfast wasn't much. But it satisfied the urgings of her empty stomach. She drank the remainder of her milk and began to stow everything back in the canvas bag. The mess kit clattered loudly against the rocks as she rinsed it out. Too loudly, she thought, reminding herself of Isaac's shadowy presence somewhere in the forest above her. His behavior confused her. She could have trusted the Isaac of summers past, could even have explained to him that she had run away and needed his help. But now his actions frightened her. He had warned her away from the lake and her island, threatened her, in fact, and now he had come here himself. Perhaps he was involved in Jim's disappearance. It was possible that he had taken Jim hostage, as Constable Allyn had said, and brought him here to an island he knew was uninhabited.

Delia sat back on her heels and looked up into the forest. If Isaac was as hostile and dangerous as everyone said, she could not risk his finding her on the island. She had hidden on the launch to get here, away from the mainland and Maggie, and perhaps in the process to help Jim. But she could accomplish nothing holed up where she was. She would have to search the island, spying on Isaac until he gave himself and his intentions away. She packed her things out of sight beneath the rocks and tied the boat beneath the birches, weighting it with rocks. There was no way to conceal it completely, short of deflating it. And Delia wanted to have it available if she needed it. Then she set off cautiously into the woods.

Isaac had moored the launch at the western end of the island. The land sloped upward to its highest point at the eastern tip, where the cottage was built. Below this crest, at mid-island, was a sort of bluff, a rounded height that broke off sharply on each side. The saddle of the bluff was wooded and thick with brush. A trail led from it to the crest of the island, a white mound of granite shot with slits of brown and gold, banked by a full stand of pine.

There had not been many trespassers, Delia thought, as she moved away from the shore, working her way across the island toward the far end, where the cottage and boathouse were. There were no film wrappers in the brush, no beer tabs or rusty cans, no signs of human beings at all. Delia stopped at every rush of squirrels in the trees, at every snapping of twigs in the underbrush, looking as often behind her as she did in front. She saw no trace of Isaac, or his wolves.

Though the island was small, tracking across it was slow going. It was late morning before Delia approached the rocky crest where the cabin was built. She paused there, under cover of the trees, where she could see the clearing around the cabin and the dock and water below. She heard the familiar lake sounds of birds, the calls of the loons, the drone of a motor in the distance, coming closer. As she watched, a boat swung into the bay, a sleek white fiberglass speedboat that left a wide V of white water in its wake. It slowed as it entered the channel, then slipped out of sight. Delia turned her attention to the cottage.

The A-frame faced east, overlooking the channel and the large bay. Its natural-shingle siding had weathered to a silvery gray, so that it blended into the greens and browns of the woods that surrounded it. But no glass was exposed to reflect the light and color of the woods. Heavy shutters covered the rear windows, screwed in place behind wide bars of wood, giving the building a blinded, crippled appearance. After three years of solitude, it looked uninhabited, uncared for. Slipping from tree to tree, Delia made her way closer, then eased around toward the front, staying close to the wall and boarded-up windows. The wide deck was littered with fallen leaves and twigs; the hummingbird feeder hung still and empty in front of the kitchen window. Delia was about to start up the steps when it registered. The shutters had been removed from the kitchen window. The slab of plywood that covered the screen door was gone, too, set aside and leaning against the wall, and the padlock that had held it shut hung open on the latch. Someone was using the cottage.

Delia glanced quickly around the clearing, listening for any sound of movement. Then, flattening herself against the wall, she slipped over to the window and inched up to peek inside.

131

TEN 🌿

A kerosene lamp glowed in the shadowed, shuttered room. Stacked and draped along the walls were clots of furniture, misshapen blobs like monsters crouched to spring upon unwary prey. Piled near the door of the cottage were strapped bundles like haystacks. Only a few feet from Delia, opposite the kitchen window, a man sat at the lamplit table, facing a cot that had been drawn up along the wall. The man sat with his back to the window, tilting his chair back on two legs. A rifle rested easily across his knees, aimed casually at the cot. A person was lying there, face in shadow, right leg roughly splinted from knee to ankle. In the lamplight Delia could see the blue swelling of the foot, resting on a folded blanket on the bare mattress of the cot. With a muted groan, the injured man pressed himself to a sitting position, propped on his elbows. It was Jim.

132

"All right, mister, no fast moves," the man in the chair said, gripping the rifle.

"Why don't you put that thing away," Jim answered, his voice tight with pain and irritation. "I'm not going anywhere."

"My orders are to take no chances." But he eased back in the chair, rocking slightly, and swung one foot up on the kitchen table, comfortably balanced. Delia could not see his face—only the weathered, dirty crown of his khaki hat, the back of his checkered wool shirt and the worn leather boat shoe on his foot.

"They're stupid orders," Jim Marshall said. "You should have left me where I was. I'd have been no trouble to you."

"Depends on how much you heard. Too bad nobody warned you about the rocks. They get slippery at night, with the dew."

"It wasn't the dew on the slippery rocks that did the damage. It was the crack on the head." Jim rubbed his hand gingerly over the back of his head. "My footing was fine until then."

The man chuckled. "But we couldn't leave you lying there on the rocks with a broken leg. Guides are supposed to help people."

"You know that this is aggravated assault, not to mention kidnapping."

The man shrugged.

"Take me back now and you'll get off easy."

"My boss wouldn't like that."

"You bet he wouldn't. Up to now you've taken all the risks for him. It isn't worth it, you know that. They'll find me. They found the game warden, and they'll find me."

"Not that search party. Not alive. They won't be looking here. And even if they did, they wouldn't find any more than they did the last time. The boss will see to that."

"You must want your share pretty bad to take this kind of chance. You're talking about murder."

"So? There's been one already, and we're still free and clear. If the boss had had his way, you'd have been the second. We won't get caught."

"That's what they all say." Jim sounded almost amused by the hackneyed familiarity of his own comment. "Statistically you're wrong, of course. You will get caught. And your boss isn't the one they'll hang for any killing that's been done."

"You better shut up now, mister." The man spoke softly, softly and threateningly. His chair thumped down on all fours and he started to get up. His long frame unbent, and he stood over Delia's stepfather. Delia pressed her cheek close to the window frame, trying to identify him. He was familiar, one of the guides—Joshua, she thought, who had given the wolf pup to Isaac. He began to turn toward the window.

Delia dropped out of sight, flattening herself against the wall, pressing closer to the danger in order to avoid it. She could hear him at the sink above her. He ran the water, shut it off, set a glass down on the counter. The boat shoes sounded a soft scuff on the wood floors as he moved away. Staying as close as she could to the wall, crouching in the tall grass that had grown up around the cabin, Delia headed for the cover of the woods. Images from dated Westerns flashed through her mind, the good guys crashing through windows, hurling flaming lamps and rescuing victims against overwhelming odds. But Delia had no weapon, and she couldn't expect any assistance from Jim. With his swollen, purple, splinted leg, he could barely move. At least he was alive. Relief pumped through her, making Delia's elbows and knees wobbly as she ducked through the weeds. But to rescue him she'd have to have help. She was no match for Joshua, much less Joshua and Isaac. She looked toward the forest, into the deep concealing greenness of the underbrush, and then back to the cottage. The shuttered windows hid any activity within, and also hid Delia from view.

She felt in the pocket of her Windbreaker. The matches were still there. Behind her in the woods were clusters of saplings, a ready supply of green wood. She could build a signal fire directly behind the cottage, on the rocks of the clearing, without being seen, and feed it with enough green wood to fill the sky above Ghost Bay with smoke. Smoke by day, her father had told her, and a blazing fire by night to mark your location when you're lost in the woods. Constable Allyn's search party couldn't miss it. It would draw them ashore and up to the cottage without warning Jim's captor. Delia could watch the rescue and hide under the birches on the shore until everyone had left. Nodding to herself, she pulled out her knife and began cutting branches and gathering kindling.

She tried to work quickly, but it took a long time to gather the leaves, the twigs and small dead branches, and then to cut the green saplings and pile their branches on the pyre. As she moved from the shelter of the trees to the rocky crest, Delia glanced often at the cottage, at the shutters that were bleached and weathered by rain and sun. But no one appeared, and the shuttered squares of window remained blank and sightless. The island, too, was quiet, in the lull of afternoon, and the lake was flat and still. Once Delia thought she heard the drone of a motor and voices, but she saw no one. As the afternoon wore on, the sky changed from the clear blue of morning to a pale, almost colorless white, with streaks of cloud. At the horizon, barely visible above the treetops, was a thin line of heavy gray clouds that spread in a slow, dark stain down from the north.

At last the fire was ready to light. Delia waited at the edge of the woods, watching the cottage carefully. When she was sure no one was watching her, she slipped over to the stack of wood. She was crouched there, behind the mound of green branches she had piled over the dead wood, when she heard the stamp of footsteps on the deck of the cottage, hurried, thumping footsteps that came toward the clearing.

"There," someone shouted. "Back in the woods! Shoot, will you, shoot!"

Delia jumped up and ran for the woods, plunging back into its cover. She was not sure if she'd been seen, or if something else was the hunter's target. She scrambled away from the cottage toward the sloping bank of the island. Slipping on the grass and moss, she tumbled over the edge. Her momentum carried her some ten feet before she could stop, grasping the rough trunk of a pine that angled out over the water. Delia clung to it, catching her breath, then looked back up toward the clearing. It was quiet, the deep quiet she had sensed before, the moment of pause between hunter and hunted. Her breath came in short, shallow gulps. After dark on summer nights at home, playing hide-and-seek in shadowy backyards, she'd felt an unreasonable terror of being caught, and had had to remind herself that it was only a game. But there were no street lights here on the island to signal an end to game playing, no mother to call her in to the yellow safety of home. Delia had left that last measure of security when she left Maggie asleep in the cottage on the mainland. Delia was alone, her trail clearly marked by the torn-up moss and grass and the broken branches of her flight down the slope. And the hunter was somewhere above her, waiting.

Bracing herself against the tree, Delia pushed herself forward and up, trying to see into the clearing. The tops of the trees that surrounded the rocky crest swayed against the white sky. The wind was rising, sounding a steady note through the branches. Delia's skin tingled with a primitive sixth sense of danger. Then something caught her eye.

The long grasses at the western edge of the clearing moved. Delia strained to make out a shape among the blurring patterns of light and dark. Touched by the shifting sunlight, even the rocks seemed to move, creeping like grotesque slugs down the slope toward her. Something was there in the tree-quickened shadows. Delia sensed more than saw it, an emptiness moving through the trees, pausing at the edge of the clearing, its form shrouded by the flickering light. She watched until her eyes blurred, and almost missed the movement on her right.

Someone was stalking up from the east. Delia heard the snap of a footstep from the direction of the cottage, along the edge of the clearing. Another careless snapping twig broke the silence, and almost simultaneously a gray blur burst from the bushes. With a low snarl the wolf lunged across the clearing, its claws scraping on the white granite of the rock as it leaped forward. Delia threw herself against the earthy slope, digging her fingers into its crisp greenness, pressing her face hard onto the prickly undergrowth. The wolf charged past above her. She heard a report, a loud pop like a firecracker, and then another, and the snarls of the wolf ceased.

Delia lay still, her back tingling with the expectation of attack. The wind was blowing strongly now, and the sky had clouded over. But nothing came down the slope after her, neither man nor beast, and no further sounds came from the clearing. Delia raised her head. Above her she heard the muted chirping of birds. She brushed the tendrils of moss and grass from her face and looked up.

The wolf lay facing her, its body stretched across the hard white stone. It did not appear to be hurt, but rather resting, lying there in the bright sun. Its tongue hung out, panting, and its chest heaved. A shiver rippled the thick gray fur, and the animal's paws twitched. Its yellow eyes focused on the woods where Delia hid. She could see the gleam of the irises, and the black slits of the wolf's pupils. Its immobility did not diminish the menace in its powerful jaws and teeth, yet Delia felt a surge of pity for it. Something was wrong. It should not be lying there in the open, unprotected. Then Delia saw the thin stream of blood at the corner of the wolf's mouth.

Impulsively she moved forward to help, to comfort the animal somehow. She had barely reached the level of the clearing when Isaac ran crouching out of the forest. He knelt beside the wolf, lifting its head to rest on his knees.

"Lobo," he said, like the sad, soft moan of the forest wind. Then, resting both palms on the thick, pale coat, he raised his eyes and looked at the sky. A moment later he had drawn his knife. Before Delia realized his intent, he slipped his hand under Lobo's jaw, pulling the throat taut, and slit his knife across it in one swift and deadly stroke.

139

Delia gasped as the wolf's blood bubbled onto the rock, running down and staining the pure white stone. Impossibly, Lobo's chest continued to strain for air, though the rise and fall of his ribs was shallow. Isaac remained on his knees, his knife unsheathed in his hand, watching the red stream pulse out and mat the wolf's white ruff. Slowly the gleam of the yellow eyes dimmed and faded. The wolf shuddered, a tremor that rippled the length of its body, and lay still, its eyes filmed over with the milky pale of death. Delia watched no more.

She thrust herself up from the earth, snatching at the pine for balance as she staggered around it, away from Isaac, away from the corpse on the bloody rock. Half sitting, half standing, she let herself slide and tumble on down the slope, too stunned with fear and death to muffle the sound of her movements or cover her trail. Branches cut at her face and arms, and she swiped at the tears of pain and shock that ran down her cheeks. When the land smoothed and leveled under a stand of pines, she stopped, fell on her hands and knees and vomited, retching until her sides ached and her throat was sore. She crawled to the water's edge and washed her face, then rinsed her mouth. Numbed by what she had seen, she had lost all sense of time and place. She stared out at the lake, gray now under a heavy sky, and watched as large drops of rain began to fall, making a pattern of circles on the smooth surface. The circles enlarged, touching against others, covering the water with bull's-eye designs as the rain increased. Delia stood there until the water was alive with the beat of the rain, watching the lake water leap up to meet the falling drops. Her hair was wet and her body shook, chilled by the rain and wind. She raised her face and closed her eyes, letting the full force of the rain wash over her, until she could no longer taste the salt of her own tears on her lips. Then she turned toward the western end of the island. Staying close to the shore, she made her way toward her camp and escape in her inflatable raft.

The rain drummed on the rocks and the water, the slippery stones echoed her steps like a ghostly tracker, but Delia did not look back. Wet branches brushed against her, and brambles and blackberry bushes tore at her hands and clothes. The shore twisted and curved far more than she remembered, with no sign of the clump of birches where her boat was hidden. The darkness of the rain was deepened by the coming of evening. Twilight had closed over the lake by the time Delia came around the last inlet and spotted the mossy bank of her hiding place. Her mind had lost all focus but the need to be away from Isaac, to reach safety and help. She ducked under the overhanging branches of the birches, threw the rocks out of the raft, untied it and slipped it into the water. It bobbed and slid on the rain-battered lake, rolling with the waves. Delia tossed in her canvas bag, retrieved the oars and jammed them through the rubber oarlocks. With one foot on the shore, she stepped into the raft, leaning on the stiff, rounded rim, and pushed off.

The wind and water pressed down on the inflatable

boat, tossing it on the increasing waves, beating against Delia's rowing. She set her course for the channel to the east where she might encounter a boat, or even spot someone from the search party. It was hard rowing. The waves were high, not like ocean waves with a regular pattern, but unpredictable, slapping at all sides of the boat at once. Somehow she made progress. But passing out of the island's protection, her raft was hit by the full force of the wind. Within minutes Delia was sitting in an inch of water. Waves jostled her, making it impossible for her to row evenly, and rain and spray pelted her face. She could no longer see the shore, which appeared as a dark area in the streaming mass of the storm. More and more the raft buckled as she rowed, wallowing uncontrollably. She straightened her legs and pressed her feet against the end of the raft, trying to steady it. But the sides continued to fold as she rowed.

Waves poured in upon her. The wind twirled the boat, driving her hard back toward the island. Through the sheets of rain gleamed the white crest of rock, the slope of its treed saddle looming darkly below it. Waves began to swirl over the wrinkled sides of the raft. There was a rumble of thunder, heavy and close, followed by a slash of lightning. In its clear and bleaching light, Delia saw that her boat was no more than an inch above the surface of the water. She pulled on the oars, trying to gain some control over her direction. The wind and waves tumbled her now toward the open bay, and now back into the channel. But the raft would not respond. It was limp, swamped by water. In the next flash of lightning Delia saw why. Where the air nozzle should have been there was only a plastic stump. Someone had cut it off, knowing that the safety plug would hold just long enough to allow her to reach deep water.

That moment of light was all Delia had to get her bearings. Thrown back into the rainswept grayness, she pulled off her shoes and parka, shoved them into the drenched canvas sack and slung it over her shoulder. Seconds later she was ducked into the icy lake, the raft sinking beneath her.

In Advanced Lifesaving, Delia had had to dive to the bottom of the pool, retrieve a weight and swim with it to poolside. She was a good swimmer, but now the weight of the sodden canvas bag dragged her down. She wallowed in the troughs of waves. When she tried to take a breath, the wind caught it, or swiped an unruly wave across her face. She intended to strike out for the nearest shore, keeping the wind behind her. But she could make out no clear direction. The shoreline was invisible in the rush of rain. The wind seemed to come from all sides, buffeting her with waves.

"I've got to keep going," she mumbled, treading water as she tried to get her breath and correct her course. Her denims weighted down her lower body, dragging her under. Holding her breath, she pulled open the snap and zipper and slipped them off, rolling them into a pillow with the air trapped inside them. Thunder   143 cracked and lightning streaked the sky, revealing once more the white rocky crest of the island. Any shore was safer than the open lake. Clutching her jeans and canvas bag in front of her for support, Delia rolled on her stomach and began kicking, aiming for the gleaming mass she had seen in the glow of the last lightning. She might have been on a treadmill of water for all the progress she made. The storm enveloped her, blotting out all sense of direction and purpose. Her arms and legs felt weighted. Exhausted, she continued to kick, to paddle, to float mindlessly on the endless lake, though she had lost all hope of reaching shore.

"I must keep going," she breathed in time to her kick. "I must keep going . . . going . . . going. . . ."

Suddenly her toe grazed something solid, jarring her out of her trance. She dropped both feet, searching for the solidity of the lake bottom and safety. But it was gone. Delia pressed forward, now veering to the left, now to the right in search of the shore. Just when she thought she'd passed it, that she had touched only a submerged tree trunk, her knee cracked against a rock and her fingers grasped at its slippery, algae-covered surface. She hung there a moment. Then slowly she began to pull herself along the rocks and out of the churning water.

Rocks rose up on either side, mere shadows in the rain. The shore around them was sandy, about two feet wide, and narrowed toward a central channel. Delia dragged herself through the shallow water and up onto the sand. Stumbling forward, she fell full length on the beach. It was dry. And the rain no longer beat on her back. Around her it was utterly, silently black. Her hand trembled and her elbow bent weakly as she reached out to the right, touching only the powdery, dry crystals of sand. She inched forward, groping to each side. Her fingernails scraped on stone. A wall of stone angled up from the sand to her right in an arch above her head. Delia crawled further, until she was stopped by a rear wall of rock.

It's a cave, she thought. *I'm in a cave*. With the last of her strength, she pulled the sodden canvas bag up beside her and curled around it in an exhausted stupor.

Delia had no sense of how much time had passed when she came to, chilled and shivering in her wet clothes. She could hear the rush of wind outside the cave and the steady drum of the rain on the rocks. Disoriented and stiff with cold, she sat up, brushed the sand from her hands and face and tried to see out the cave's opening. Everything was dark or light gray—the sides of the cave, the sky outside, the sand. Her thoughts came slowly, as though her brain had been sapped and paralyzed by her battle with the storm.

Remembering the canvas bag, she fumbled with the knotted drawstring, opened it and dumped the contents out around her. Her parka and shoes were dripping wet, but the matches were still in her pocket, wrapped tightly in plastic. Something heavy rolled toward her foot. The flashlight. Delia picked it up, shook it and

145

switched it on. The beam faltered, but it worked, revealing a low cavern. Its mouth was no more than three feet wide, but the cave curved back over an area about ten feet across that was divided by a stream entering from the lake and disappearing behind the rear wall. The ceiling was low, so that Delia could not stand upright. She pointed the light upward, shining it on the rough stone. In all her years of visiting the island, she had never discovered this cave. With its entrance hidden by the high water, it was not visible from the lake, nor from the shore. Yet it had been here since the island's formation, pressed up beneath the granite ridge like a partially submerged cup.

She dropped the beam of light down along the sides of the cave entrance to the sandy beach and small stream. The water lapped softly at her feet, calm in the face of the rain outside. Broken pieces of driftwood lay on the sand at its mouth. It took only minutes to gather them up, strip off the bark for tinder and break off the twigs for kindling. Delia laid the fire carefully; then, with her back to the cave opening and the wind, she struck a match and held it to the small pile of tinder. The bark curled away from the heat, the match burned down toward her fingers. The fire caught. Tiny flutters of flame spread upward, whispering around the twigs and dry wood, and finally crackling them into ashes.

Delia sat back on her heels and held her hands out to the small blaze, warmed as much by the sight of its

yellow flickering as by the heat it gave off. Streaks of

mica in the cave wall caught the light and reflected it in glittering sparks. The stone itself absorbed the heat as the fire burned more steadily and warmed the air in the cave. Sheltered from the rain and wind, snug and warm for the first time since the weather had changed, Delia was able to think. She had lost her boat and failed to rescue Jim or escape from Isaac. But she had not drowned, and she had dry, safe lodging for the night. Before she could do anything else, she had to rest, and eat. Carefully she examined the contents of the canvas bag, discarding the soggy crackers and cereal, and the dissolved packets of milk. She was able to salvage the jar of peanut butter, the dried fruit and a candy bar. From the bottom of the bag she took the rain poncho, a large square of nylon with an opening and hood at the center. Stripping off the rest of her clothes, Delia wrapped herself in the poncho. She draped her Windbreaker and blue jeans over pieces of driftwood stuck in the sand around the fire and spread the other things on the sand to dry. Huddled close to the flames, she ate some peanut butter and raisins. With her hunger somewhat satisfied, she lay back on the soft sand in the steamy warmth of the cave. Isaac and Jim and Maggie, the island itself, seemed very far away, all part of a separate world. It was hours until dawn, she thought, hours before she would be hunted again. She closed her eyes.

ELEVEN 🌿

Delia woke with a start. Embers glowed where her fire had been. The entrance to the cave was a bright circle of sunlight. The storm had passed, leaving the lake rippled and sparkling. From where she lay on the sandy floor of the cave, Delia could see the hazy green of a distant shore between the pale blue of the morning sky and the deeper blue-green of the lake. The arc of the cave entrance was like a window. It reminded Delia of a long-ago Easter gift, an egg made of crystallized sugar with glass in one end and a tiny scene displayed inside. The fragile immobility of that interior both fascinated and dismayed Delia. Sometimes she would set the egg on the shelf in her room at just the right angle so that she could look into it unexpectedly, and perhaps witness the droop of a sugary flower petal, the twitch of a bunny's ear. But it never changed from its lifeless, saccharine perfection and became for her at last a curiosity to observe rather than a world to enter.

148

The lake beyond the cave sparkled with vitality, but was as remote from her as the sugar egg. This was the lake as Delia remembered it, the place she had come to renew her memory of her father. She had come to find not a window, but a door to that memory, a way to enter into it again. Instead she found herself trapped in a dim cave, on an island of unexpected, unfamiliar contours.

Delia pushed herself up and crawled stiffly over to the stream to wash her face. Without the heat from the fire, the air in the cave had cooled. The fresh breeze from outside was crisp and bracing. Quickly Delia gathered up her clothes. Her denim pants were still damp, but her underwear and socks and sweater had dried. She pulled them on and slipped her feet into her shoes. The canvas was dry and stiff, but inside her sneakers were damp and spongy. When she was dressed she took out the peanut butter and dried fruit. She ate slowly, deciding what to do, putting off as long as possible her exit from the cave. Here at least she felt safe, sitting with her back to the stone wall and facing the only access to the cave. Whatever danger came she would meet head on. But she could not remain in hiding. She had to get back to her green-wood fire. If she could not leave the island to get help, she would have to signal for it, and hope it arrived in time. With a shudder, she put aside the thought that it might already be too late for Jim, and prepared to leave. Just thinking about climbing back up to the clearing made her breath come in short, rapid gulps that echoed in the dim cave.

She paused, listening, then swallowed and held her breath. The slow inhalations continued. A whispered panting filled the cave. Delia was not alone. A chill of fear rippled up her back, and she pressed herself hard against the rough stone. Something moved outside, just beyond the rocks. Delia pulled her canvas bag close with one hand, gripped the flashlight in the other. She watched as a gray mass detached itself from the rocks. Moving on long, delicate legs, the gray wolf entered the cave. Slowly it stepped onto the sandy beach and sniffed the air, turning its head toward Delia. Inch by inch Delia straightened up against the wall. Rea was smaller than Lobo had been, but still powerfully built. Yellow eyes slanted back in her head, and her ears pricked back and forth, flickering for sounds. The fire might have kept Delia safe, but its glow of embers was no threat now to the wolf. Delia raised the flashlight, moving her arm in fractions of inches.

No fast movements, she told herself, *and don't show that you're afraid.* Staring directly at the wolf, she snapped on the beam, aiming for Rea's eyes. The animal crouched and its ears dropped back and down. Delia started to edge away from it, and it drew its lips back in a soundless snarl. Delia took another step. The wolf stood still, but uttered a low, rumbling growl. Holding the light steady, Delia moved again to her right. With the light full in her eyes, Rea flattened her ears against her head. This time she snarled aloud, a deep and heavy threat that echoed in the small rocky chamber.

"Back, Rea!"

The voice so startled Delia that she nearly dropped the flashlight. At the mouth of the cave, silhouetted against the clear sky, stood Isaac. One hand was poised on his knife, the other he held straight up, palm flat, toward the wolf.

"Don't move," he said to Delia. "She'll be all right if you just don't move."

He ducked under the stone archway and, stooping, laid his hand on Rea's head. She whined, flicking her ears and looking up at him.

"Down," he commanded. Reluctantly the wolf gathered her hind legs under her and sat. Delia had remained where she stood, crouched against the rear wall of the cave, as Isaac approached the wolf. She saw him touch the wolf's head, his gesture one of complete control, as restraining as a chain around Rea's neck. When Isaac looked down at the animal, Delia slipped sideways away from him, shrinking along the cave wall. Still training the flashlight on the wolf, Delia stretched her free hand out along the rocks, groping for an escape, a weapon. Her fingertips scraped the rock, scratching harshly against its indentations, following its contours. Suddenly it gave way.

Delia wrenched her gaze from Isaac and the wolf, and looked to her right. From only a foot away, the wall appeared to be solid but actually dropped back in an acute curve that formed a narrow passage out of the cave. Without thinking about where it might lead, Delia darted into it. The sandy bank fell away sharply, but she still had to crouch to avoid hitting her head on the low-hanging rocks of the ceiling. The beam of the flashlight bounced from wall to wall as she ran. She needed both hands to keep her balance through the tunnel that curved ahead of her like a swirl of water. The rubber soles of her shoes slipped on the slate that had replaced the sandy cave floor. Stumbling, she stepped forward and plunged into icy water, knee deep. The stream that disappeared beneath the rear wall of the cave reemerged here and probably had cut the passage through the rock. Delia flashed her light down in front of her, and then to each side.

What she had thought was the back of the cave was really a false wall that curved like a buttressing arm through the center of a large cavern. In years when the lake was high, water would fill the cave and submerge it, covering its entrance. But now, at low water, it left an empty, echoing chamber. The rocky walls curved up in rounded slopes a good twelve feet above Delia's head. In front of her, covering most of the floor of the cavern, was a lagoon about fifteen feet across. Directly opposite Delia, at the far limit of her flashlight beam, the cave walls split into a narrow inverted V that opened onto the south side of the island. Delia splashed out of the water up onto the bank and began to run toward it.

The slate bank of the lagoon was slippery with algae, and Delia skidded on it as she ran. The corners of the cavern were shadowy and rank with rotting vegetation, with weeds and lake grasses and pieces of fallen trees that had been driven by storms into the cavern and left there when the water level dropped. The sticks seemed to be piled against the walls in stacks, with an occasional loose branch poking out to trip her. Delia plunged on. She had come nearly to the southern entrance when she heard Isaac behind her. Instinctively, she turned to face him when he shouted, swinging her light along the eastern wall, past the passage opening, to spotlight Isaac at the edge of the lagoon.

"Wait," he called. "Where are you going? Don't go out there!" He was reaching out toward her, one arm extended as though he could pluck her from the rocks back into the cave. Frightened as she was, the warning in his voice made her turn and look out at the water, in expectation of attack from that direction. There was nothing but the expanse of the lake glittering in the sunlight and, softly, at a distance, the growl of a motor on the open bay. Poised on the rocks at the mouth of the cave, Delia heard the sound clearly. It was the drone of an approaching boat, a large boat, and it was headed toward the channel.

Delia looked back at Isaac. He had stepped forward, away from the cave wall, and was looking over his shoulder at the stack of twigs and branches. Delia's light played over it, catching Isaac and the pale gleam of limbs stripped of bark. Delia wobbled slightly, losing traction on the rocks. Her light dipped, falling on a round white bole of wood at Isaac's feet. But it was not

153

wood. It was bone—round and smooth with two gaping sockets. Isaac jerked back from the skull and looked again at Delia, to see if she had recognized the grisly thing. Stacked behind him were bones, not the innocent leavings of the lake, but the bones of animals trapped and slaughtered for skins and heads and antlers.

"Here?" Isaac stared at the remains of the creatures that lay in heaps at his feet. His hands clenched into fists at his sides. "All the time I watched, they were adding to their kill. All that time the proof was here and I couldn't find it. They were killing and I was doing nothing, and now it's too late."

He stepped closer to the wall, reaching out as though he would tear the bones from their resting place and cast them out of sight, out of existence and memory into the dark waters of the lagoon. Instead, he knelt and drew out the desiccated, mutilated carcass of an eagle, its remaining feathers flattened and lifeless. For a moment Isaac bent his head over it, then stood up and scanned the cave. The poachers had dumped no dead bodies recently along the rocky walls. The cavern was damp and musty, but not corrupt with the odor of decaying flesh.

"And they're still free," Isaac declared. "Free to be paid for their dirty business. They'll be paid this time, I swear it."

His hand fell on the sheathed knife at his belt. He seemed to have forgotten Delia, and, stunned, she had remained at the mouth of the cave. She stepped back now, rattling pebbles beneath her feet. Isaac turned. Across the black surface of the lagoon they stared at one another for a moment. Then Delia stumbled back, out of the cave and onto the south shore of the island.

She headed up the slope, climbing onto the rise that was the outside roof of the cave. She tore at the brush, pulling herself up toward the clear sunlight, driven by fear and horror at what lay behind her in the cave. If she could climb the rock and reach the crest of the island, she would have some chance of signaling for help before Isaac caught up with her. She could hear him behind her, splashing through the lagoon. Sliding on the rough rock, she kept running uphill. Shale and loose rock crumbled under her wet shoes; her clothes caught on brush and brambles as she scrambled up. Panting, she came out on level ground—the saddle of land at the center of the island. Above her loomed the sheer face of white granite topped by pines, blue-black in the sharp sun. Delia scanned the rock for a path, but its smooth, sloping base was littered after the night's storm with fallen branches and broken trees that blocked the way. A huge pine had been toppled from the stand on the crest of the island and lay across the saddle. Its heavy, soil-laden roots hung brokenly over the cliff above the lake.

On the hillside Delia heard the snap and rustle of Isaac's movements. He would catch up with her in moments, unless she could trick him into thinking that she had gone ahead. Quickly she yanked aside some of the debris on the path, then jumped behind the pine and huddled in its branches, her back to the cliff and the lake. Only moments later she saw the top of Isaac's head emerge from the brush on the slope. Before he had edged any farther onto the level saddle, Delia swung her canvas bag around in a swooping arc and let it fly, sending it sailing up into the growth on the crest of the hill. Ducking under the branches, Delia squinted through the pungent, green needles. Isaac turned toward the stony crest, toward the snapping tumble of the canvas bag down the hillside. Shoving through the broken branches and chunks of rock, he started up the path, out of Delia's sight.

She waited until her breath came in even drafts instead of smothered pantings. Soon enough Isaac would realize she was not on the hill and return to search her out. To go back the way she had come was to chance meeting Rea. Nor could she follow Isaac up the path. There was only one way down from the saddle. Delia twisted her body to look over the edge of the cliff on which she and the pine tree balanced. The drop to the water was about twenty feet. The lake was calm enough, but it gave no hint of the jagged rocks that might lie beneath its surface. Delia's palms dampened in sudden fear. She could not muster the courage to jump off the twelve-foot platform at the community pool, much less leap from this height into waters possibly cluttered with boulders.

156   *But if I jumped, I'd come out on the northeastern tip of the*

island, she told herself, *close to the boathouse. I could get to the signal fire that way.*

She crept on her hands and knees to the edge of the cliff and peered over. Pebbles broke from under her palms. They fell a long way before splashing into the water below. Delia shivered at the thought of leaping into the cold, unknown water. Her stomach turned, and she closed her eyes against the vertigo that dizzied her. Poised high above the blue-gray lake in the pine branches, Delia gathered her feet under her, looked down once, then tensed her muscles to spring out into the clear air.

"Don't move!" The harsh whisper came from her left. Isaac's black eyes gleamed out at her from the bushes, the flat slabs of his cheekbones smeared with dirt. In his right hand the unsheathed knife glittered silver and sharp. Delia's breath burst from her in a thin, wavering cry. She pushed back against the pine to run, to jump, to escape in any way from the filleting knife and the hard, brown hand that reached out for her. Pressured by her weight, the tree shivered, its balance shifting. Delia hesitated at the cliff edge an instant too long. The tree moved, slipping at first slowly, then gathering speed. Its wet, heavy branches tangled and whipped around her legs, snapping them out from under her. Flat on her face suddenly, her pants legs caught in the sticky, coarse wood, Delia felt the pine sliding backward over the cliff, pulling her with it. With a rush of needles, it teetered on the edge of the twenty-foot drop, then tilted and with a groan plunged down toward the lake. Scrabbling for a grip on the loose rock as she was swept backward, Delia screamed and Isaac leaped, his knife outstretched. He slashed at her denims, tearing at them with his bare hands to free her from the tree, then fell on top of her. The long arms of the tree battered and tugged at them as the pine hurtled down toward the water. Only Isaac's weight kept them on the cliff edge. Delia's legs dangled limply over the water as the tree crashed down, spearing into the black, rock-strewn depths of the lake.

❧TWELVE

Delia was only dimly aware of Isaac's scooping her up and carrying her to the base of the bluff. There was a drumming in her ears that blocked out everything around her. He set her down in the rocky shade, with her back braced against the granite. Then, gently but firmly, he pressed her head forward between her knees and steadied her there. Slowly the drumming subsided. Delia blinked at the chips of stone at her feet and watched them come into focus. A sprig of pine needles was stuck in her shoelace. As her faintness receded, the rush in her ears gave way to a different beating, a mechanical throbbing that was external to her. A boat was running slowly below them along the side of the island.

"There, did you hear that? Someone's up there."

Delia recognized her mother's voice. Maggie was there, just below them on the cliff edge, near enough so that Delia could hear her. Delia's throat ached with

159

an unuttered shout, but she could not afford to bungle the only chance she might have of signaling the boat.

"You must have heard it," Maggie repeated. "Someone screamed. There's someone on that island."

"I can't say I did hear it, Mrs. Marshall." It was a man who spoke, probably young McPherson, Delia thought. "You saw that tree fall," he went on. "Those branches make lots of noise when they rub together like that. It might even sound like a human voice."

"It was a human voice."

"Now, Miss Maggie, you can't be all that sure." This was a different, older voice. Mr. Mac and his son must be in the boat with her mother, Delia decided. She listened, trying to judge how close to the shore they were.

"Sometimes, when you want to hear something," the old man was saying, "you convince yourself that you did hear. Believe me, I've done it myself."

"And the whole lake knows about the times you've done it," McPherson said, sneering at his father. "We found the remains of your daughter's raft, Mrs. Marshall. There's no way she got to shore in one piece in that storm."

"She's a fine swimmer. She might have made it."

"But the chances are she didn't. I don't mean to be brutal about it," McPherson said, denying his effect. "But we have to face the facts. Let me take you back to the resort. We'll keep looking. You need to rest."

"Mr. McPherson," Maggie addressed him with gritty
160 patience. She sounded tired, but determined, as if all

vagueness had been leached out of her by the strain of Delia's and Jim's disappearances. "This is the only place in the immediate area you haven't searched for my husband. This is where Delia would have tried to come. That we found her raft only proves my point. I am not going back to the mainland until I set foot on this island and see for myself that they are not here."

"If they are, we'll find them, Miss Maggie," Mr. Mac insisted. "There's no need for you to put yourself through this."

"Yes, there is. I never should have agreed to come back here, but I let myself be talked into it. Now I can't leave until I've seen for myself everything I believed I should never have to see again."

She paused as though she heard her own words for the first time when she spoke them, and had to consider them as they settled before her in the storm-cleared air. Mr. Mac began to protest again, but his son broke in.

"If Mrs. Marshall insists, we'll take her ashore."

"Are you crazy? We can't do that," the old man argued. Even at that distance Delia could hear his agitation.

"We'll have to," his son answered, "if that's what she wants."

"I didn't agree to that. I mean, it might be dangerous. We don't know what we'll find there. It may not be safe."

"It's too late to worry about that now. Mrs. Marshall's made up her mind." Delia could imagine the calm, controlled face McPherson turned on his father's sput-

161

terings, the unreadable mirrored lenses of his glasses deflecting all argument. "You'd better get up forward," he ordered, "and guide me around this tree."

It was as clear an indication of their location as Delia was likely to get. She hesitated another moment, sitting still beneath the pressure of Isaac's palm. Then, putting all her weight behind a sudden swing to the left, she shoved Isaac off balance. She sprang away from him, snatching a handful of rocks from the scattering at her feet. She pitched them wildly toward the edge of the cliff and shouted. But whatever sound she made was lost beneath the cry that rose at that moment from the bowels of the island. It trembled on the still morning air, lifted and echoed back on itself. Distorted and amplified, it reverberated in the cave below them. Rea's howl stopped Delia in midstep, stunned her and stunned them all, all except Isaac. In the moment of Delia's hesitation he was beside her, his hand clamped over her mouth as he wrestled her back from the cliff edge, out of sight of the boat. Delia struggled and bit into his calloused palm. He winced, but held firm.

"Be quiet," he rasped in her ear. "Be quiet, or you'll never see your mother again."

Rea's baying continued, its rise and fall covering the sounds of their struggle. The boat moved on, swinging past the fallen tree toward the east end of the island and the dock. When it was out of sight and hearing, Isaac released Delia, jerking her around to face him.

"You little fool," he said. "Don't you know you're only safe as long as they have no idea you're here?"

"Safe? With you?" Delia faced him squarely. Her knees felt loose and wobbly, and her elbows, too. But she was no longer aware of fear, of the mouth-drying, cold panic that had driven her out of the cave and up the slope of the island away from Isaac. In his ragged clothes, face to face, Isaac and his hungry strength were not so threatening. Unexpectedly, Delia thought of Jim, helpless on the cot, yet undaunted by his captor.

"Safe, am I? From what? You may have to hide from them, but I don't. I haven't done anything. You're the only one who isn't safe."

"You don't know what you're talking about," Isaac said, watching her. "And this is no place for explanations. Come on." He grasped her wrist in his hard fingers and swung it up between her shoulder blades. Pushing her ahead of him, Isaac crossed the rocky saddle and continued down the slope of the island to the cave. He and Delia seemed to slip through solid rock into the cavern, so hidden was its entrance from the outside. Rea stood up as they entered, her baying subsiding to barks of greeting.

Isaac propelled Delia past the wolf into the cave, then let her go. "Don't try to run," he warned. "She's faster than you are." He knelt then to pat the wolf, crooning softly to her as he rubbed her ears and ruff. After a moment he stood and took from his pocket a piece of dried beef jerky.

"Stand still. Let her get to know you. She won't hurt you. Then give her this. Make friends."

Delia stood quietly with the meat in her hand, while   163

Isaac led the wolf over to her. Rea's coat was a silvery gray, white across the chest and up into her ruff. Her muzzle was also white, with a deep gray mask around her eyes. Like Lobo's, her eyes were yellow with a streak of black pupil at the center. A rim of white tipped her ears. They snapped forward now, and Rea sniffed delicately. Her skull was broad, and her shoulders were full and heavy. Her feet would leave a deep track, but she moved lightly, like a dancer or a racehorse. Her legs seemed too thin to carry her weight so gracefully. As the wolf circled her, Delia noticed that she limped slightly.

"She's hurt," she said to Isaac.

"No. Her back leg's malformed. Maybe that's why she's content to hunt close to home. She knows she can't run too far without tiring."

"Why was she howling?"

"She was calling me."

"You don't expect me to believe that." Delia looked from the wolf to Isaac.

"Wolves are pack animals, and a lot better company than people. Except for Lobo, Rea's had no one but me. So she communicates with me the way she would with a pack."

"And you answer her," Delia said. "That's what we heard that day when I saw you by the lake. You were answering her."

"Probably." Isaac pointed to the meat. "You better toss that to her. She's not a discriminating eater. Don't try to feed her from your hand or you could lose a finger. Accidentally."

"You said you would take them north and let them go, or give them to a zoo."

"They weren't ready. Or I wasn't." He was looking around the cave as they talked. "I guess this will have to do," he said, pulling off the length of leather thong he had wrapped around his waist as a belt. "Sit down."

Delia stared at him.

"Sit down. I can't have you running around loose. You and Rea will have to stay here." He measured off a length of leather and cut it. "I'll make it as comfortable for you as I can. You'll be able to move, but not far. Not far enough to leave here."

"What are you going to do?"

"I have a score to settle." Snapping the leather between his two fists to test it, he approached Delia. She backed away, bumping into the cave wall. In spite of her resolution to show no fear, her voice trembled.

"You don't have to tie me up. Rea wouldn't let me leave."

"I told you to stay out of this. I told you to go home. Now it's too late. Are you going to sit down?"

Eyes wide and focused on the leather strip, Delia slid slowly down the wall. The thought of being tied up in the dank cave, unable to protect herself against Rea or any other danger, brought her to the edge of panic. Her courage ebbed away. Suppose Isaac never came back to free her, or returned only for Rea and

165

left Delia to lie there, bound, until the lake rose again and filled the cave? Her bones would roll with its currents under the black waters of the lagoon, pounding against the slimy, algae-coated rocks until they were reduced to powder—until, like the animals already slaughtered there, she had disappeared into the cycle of the great lake.

"You don't have to keep me here," she said. "I won't tell anyone you're on the island." She swallowed against the dryness in her throat as Isaac tied a loop at each end of the leather thong. "They've probably found Jim by now, anyway. If they find me, too, they'll leave."

"That's what I'm afraid of." Isaac squatted down beside her. "They've got to be stopped."

"Stopped from what? From finding me? Wait, listen." Delia pulled away from him. "It's not me they want. It's Jim. He's the only one my mother cares about." Somehow she had to avoid being left bound and helpless in the cave. She kept talking, running her words together in rapid bursts.

"She never wants to see this place again. You heard her. She didn't want to come back. That's why I ran away. I had to get away from them, from my mother and Jim. If they find me, they'll make me go back. And I can't. I've got to stay here." Delia's urgency was sincere, with her fear that Isaac would leave her defenseless in the cave. "Once they find Jim, they'll leave."

"If they can. If they're still alive."

"What?"

Isaac held the loops of leather loose in his hands. "You don't understand yet, do you? It's McPherson. He's responsible for all of this." He swept his hands out to indicate the animal remains. "He's to blame for the killing, all of the killing. And he's got to be stopped."

Isaac's words swam toward Delia, floating through the heavy air of the cave like bubbles, noxious but true. Suddenly it all made sense—McPherson's shock at hearing who Delia and Maggie were, Mr. Mac's dismay at finding that they had returned to the lake, their efforts to keep the family away from Ghost Island, to convince her mother to sell it if possible. Even McPherson's search for Jim had been restricted to the mainland, and he'd argued with the constable to keep searchers off the lake.

"McPherson brought Jim here?" Delia's brain seemed to be working at half capacity, and her thoughts chunked into place inconsistently.

"If it hadn't been for Mr. Mac, he'd have killed him. And if it hadn't been for you, I might have stopped them then."

"Me? I didn't have anything to do with it."

"You came out to Cat Point, remember?" Isaac slipped the leather loops around her ankles. "When I heard about the game warden's murder, I knew I had to get away from here. I closed up my grandmother's house and came down to McPherson's with the wolves to steal the launch. It was the only boat big enough to get us north fast. I figured he owed me that much." 167

"And you found us."

"Right in the middle of everything. I had camped on the point until I could get to the boathouse and the launch. From what I overheard, your stepfather walked in on McPherson's meeting with Joshua, while they were planning how to clear their stuff off Ghost Island."

Angry with Maggie, Jim must have continued on down the path to Cat Point, stepping off the dark trail into the clearing, startling McPherson into more violence.

"They'd have killed him then," Isaac said, "except that Mr. Mac threatened to blow the whole operation if they did. Mr. Mac took him to the cottage instead. I was going after him when I ran into you."

Delia shivered, remembering the conversation between the McPhersons, the thud of Jim's body being tossed into the Peterboro.

"I could have helped. You didn't have to scare me like you did."

"You were in the way. There wasn't time." Isaac brushed at the air, dismissing her. "Besides, I had the wolves. I couldn't leave them on the mainland, and I had to stop McPherson, so I brought them here with me."

"And then came back to get the launch?"

Isaac nodded. "By the time I got here, Mr. Mac was gone and Joshua was guarding your stepfather. It's McPherson I want. Once I take care of him and free your stepfather, I'll head north with Rea. Fast."

168   "You can still do that," Delia stammered. "I can help."

"You? Help me? Nobody can help me." Roughly he jerked the loops tight around her ankles. "Not with what I have to do."

As the leather closed on her skin, Delia felt the space around her diminish. The weight of the island seemed to be pressing down and compressing the cave. There was less air, and the fruity smell of decomposing vegetation and mouldering bones was heavy, as if the foul odors had at last overbalanced the drift of fresh air through the narrow openings in the rock. Her skin prickled with unreasoning terror, and choking waves of panic rose in her throat. Delia forced herself to breathe evenly, to sit quietly instead of lashing out in a futile struggle with Isaac. She took a deep breath.

"What are you going to do?"

Isaac didn't answer.

"You've got to listen. I'm a witness. I can help you. You can trust me." Dismayed by the tremor in her voice, Delia leaned forward toward Isaac. "You trusted my father. You listened to him."

"For all the good it did me." He stood up. The light reflecting off the water of the lagoon flickered across the flat, broad planes of Isaac's face, twisting and contorting it with shadows. He held the other length of the leather thong wrapped around his palm. "I tried his way, and this is where it got me. If this is your justice, I want none of it. It didn't stop McPherson before, and it won't stop him now. So I will."

"No, you can't. That's murder."

169

"It's justice."

"Killing him won't change anything," Delia cried. "There'll be others to take his place."

"But he'll never kill anything again. At least I'll stop him. Hold out your hands."

"No, wait!" Delia's voice rose in desperation as Isaac's hand closed over her wrist. "Don't you care about anything?"

Isaac began to wind the leather angrily, tightly around her wrists.

"Once my people lived on this lake. We hunted on these islands, we fished this water, harvested rice from the marshes of the river. We named the fish you call the muskie, the *maskioje*, the great pike."

Delia listened, fastening on his words. As long as he was talking, there was still a chance he would not leave. Her interest tied her to him, even as he leaned over and checked the knots he'd made.

"Now the muskellunge is nearly gone. It hangs, our great pike, as a trophy on the walls of your people's homes." His words shot like arrows from a bow, tingling with anger.

"That's not my fault. I'm not like that. My father wasn't like that."

"Your people buy the land, as if they could own the earth. Your father bought this island. He built on it, changed it."

"We had to build or we'd have lost the property. That's the law, that you must build on the land within five years."

Isaac ignored her protest, jerking the knots tight at her wrists.

"Those things aren't my fault, or my father's. We didn't make the laws," Delia insisted, her voice rising. "You can't blame me or my father for them."

"Your people make the laws to suit themselves. You take what you want until there's nothing left to take. And then you leave. You'll leave behind a dead lake unless someone stops you."

"You're no better. Suppose you do kill McPherson? You'll be caught and tried. What good will that do? Will that stop the poachers and the others who'll destroy the lake?" Delia could not control a shudder as she glanced at the bones. "You were going to protect this lake. That's why you went to school. If you really cared, you'd have stuck that out and learned something."

"Nothing I learned could help. No one would listen." He stared down at the intricate pattern of the leather knots. "There would have been nothing left to protect."

"And what's left now? Nothing but bones." Delia's voice broke. "Lobo's bones."

"Lobo was dying." Isaac turned away from her.

"No," Delia cried. Her voice was high and shrill, edging out of control. Isaac spun back around to face her.

"Yes. I only spared him a slow and painful death."

Tears welled up in Delia's eyes and began to run down her cheeks, in spite of her efforts to control them. Her throat thickened with the salty taste, choking her.

"You didn't have to kill him," she sobbed, "not here. Not on my island."

"Lobo was dying." Isaac bent down and grabbed Delia's shoulders, but she turned her face away. "Can't you understand that? He was already dying. McPherson shot him."

Isaac began to shake her so hard that her head snapped back and forth.

"Couldn't you do something?" she asked, spacing her words between the rough jerking. Isaac released her, shoving her away. She flopped loosely against the stones like a rag doll.

"Lobo attacked to protect Rea and me, and McPherson shot him."

"But you could have tried." Delia's voice wobbled and cracked. Fear, exhaustion and the constraint of the leather thongs were taking their toll. "You might have saved him."

"No." Isaac rocked back on his heels. He stared past Rea, out the opening between the rocks, at the lake and the sky. "Lobo died defending his pack, Rea and me. There was nothing more to do."

The murmur of Isaac's voice faded and joined the hollow soughing of the wind and the water through the rocks. In the half-darkness of the cave, the words wavered for Delia like a refrain from the past.

"My father was dying," she said.

"Yes," Isaac answered softly. "I knew."

172   "I didn't. No one would tell me. They whispered

about it, but they never told me." The words she had said only to herself tumbled out, and Delia let them come, too tired to hold them back any longer. "Not even my mother would say it, not even when he changed. My father got sick and gray and his clothes didn't fit and his voice scraped like peeled paint. But they didn't tell me anything. He went to the hospital and he never came back. She gave his clothes away and packed up all the pictures. And then she married Jim. It was as if my father had never been. I couldn't find him anymore. That's why I had to come back here, to find him."

"He isn't here. Your father is dead."

Delia jerked back as though Isaac had slapped her.

"He has to be here. If he isn't here, he's nowhere. He's gone." She clamped her lips tight over each word to stop the torrent she had loosed. "I'd have found him here if nothing had changed. It would have been as if he'd just gone out fishing. I'd have remembered."

"You remember now."

"Only the sickness," Delia cried. "And I hated that. I hated him for being sick. I hated his dying. Here on the island I could remember him the way he used to be."

"He was both."

"No," Delia objected. "That wasn't my father. He was different. Dying made him different. It made my mother different. My mother promised we'd come back to the lake. She always kept her promises. But they wouldn't bring me here to the island, she and Jim. They said it wasn't safe. They wanted to sell the land. I told them 173 they couldn't, that I wouldn't let them. That's why I ran away."

"You shouldn't have come," Isaac said. "I told you to stay away."

"But it's mine. My father loved it here. It's all I have left."

Looking up, she saw Isaac's haunted leanness. He was not what he had been. He had changed as the lake itself had changed, revealing a darkly sinister side, as different from her memory of him as the dim recesses of the cavern were different from her memory of her island.

"I only wanted things to be the same," she said.

Isaac's eyes narrowed, gleaming like miniatures of the lagoon. "But they're not the same. Your father's dead. He didn't die on purpose, but he's gone. Let him go."

"I just want to remember him."

"No, you don't. You want a shrine. You want this." Isaac stood up and backed away, gesturing at the bones stacked along the cave walls. "You want a place where nothing ever changes."

"And you don't? What about the lake?"

"The lake isn't dead. Not yet." He turned from her and the grim evidence of the bones, and moved toward the entrance of the cave.

"Wait," Delia cried out, trying to get up as she reached out to him. "Wait, Isaac. Don't do it. Don't go."

"You'll be all right. Rea will stay with you."

At the sound of her name, the wolf whined and stood up, her ears flicking back and forth as she watched Isaac

"Down, Rea," he said, holding the flat of his hand up to her. "You stay." Isaac looked over his shoulder at Delia. "Don't try to leave. Even if you could get past Rea, you'd break your neck on the rocks with that hobble on your feet."

"What difference would that make? You don't care. Isaac, stop, please."

But Isaac only paused for an instant at the opening in the rocks. Then, without looking back, he stepped out and disappeared beyond the archway. Rea lay with her ears cocked, listening, until even she could hear no more sound from him. Then she turned her massive head to Delia, fixing on her an unblinking yellow stare.

THIRTEEN ❧

The silence was broken only by the soft panting of the wolf. The absence of another human being exaggerated Delia's awareness of the stillness in the cave, and of the hollow, reverberating emptiness. A damp chill settled over her, seeping into her joints. At first she simply stared at the opening through which Isaac had disappeared—as though watching could make him reappear —and listened, barely breathing in her effort to hear some small sound of life beyond her subterranean prison. She focused on the slice of open space in the rocks as though she could will the earth to split apart and set her free. The minutes passed, and Delia remained huddled against the wall, her knees drawn up to her chin, staring into the space around her. The surface of the lagoon glimmered over murky, unplumbed depths, and moist, crystalline chunks of rock caught the shattered light. Delia's glance skittered past them to Rea, and back to the stack of bones against the wall. Repellent as they were, she could not keep from looking at them. The pale heap of bones drew her like a magnet, as if examining the detritus of death could teach her to understand it.

She shuddered and turned away, meeting the yellow gleam of Rea's eyes in her masked, gray face, and saw again the face of the dying Lobo. His head clamped in Isaac's strong brown hands, the wolf had slipped open-eyed into death. Delia had witnessed the moment of its coming, had known the instant Lobo ceased to exist. It happened in the eyes, even before his blood had ceased to pump. The light was gone, burned out, its source extinguished. No longer Lobo, the wolf became an inert thing.

Slowly Delia looked back at the bones. That was death, the change from being to thing. The lifeless thing decayed, resolved itself into the earth. And the being became memory, gone and not gone, existing only in the minds of the living. Lobo was dead. Delia saw again his leap into the clearing, heard the shot, and saw him fall, dying, onto the island rock. In the still darkness of the cave, he was as clear to her as Rea, lying panting on the shore. But Lobo was no ghost, no half-live being imagined just outside her sight. Lobo was dead, dead yet remembered.

Delia turned away from the bones and looked into the surface of the lagoon. The light glittered in silver streaks across it, like falling stars on a night sky. If she closed her eyes and shut it out, the light would still touch and glisten on the black depths. There was no running from this place, not even if the leather thongs dropped suddenly from her hands and feet. Delia took a deep breath, raised her hands to her face and wiped away the last of her tears. She licked her dry lips.

"Let him go," Isaac had said.

"He was dying," she said aloud, tentatively. The thin whisper of her voice sounded unfamiliar in the hollow chamber. "My father was dying," she repeated, and heard the words. "My father is dead," she said.

Not a stranger, but her father with a thinner, pain-worn face, had said goodbye and left the house and died. Staring at the still, black water of the lagoon, Delia remembered hugging him before she left for school, before he left for the hospital; she had hugged him and stepped back, smiling up. His eyes had never changed, she could remember now. His eyes had remained the same. The specter of his illness faded as she recalled his eyes and saw him whole against her clearing memory. No place or person could strike the fire of life in him again, but as surely as his dust existed in the substance of the earth, he would exist in the timeless, trackless reaches of her mind. As long as she lived, he was alive—there in her memory. With that realization came a rush of relief, a new consciousness of herself. Energy jolted through her chilled, hunched limbs, and she struggled to her feet.

Her hands were numb and she had no feeling in her toes. When she looked at the cave entrance, her eyes blurred and light streaked in bright colors across them, her focus distorted by her concentration on the dark waters of the lagoon. She realized that she was still trapped under the earth, yet she no longer felt the debilitating pressure of the rocky weight above her. The opening in the rocks was not just the place where Isaac would enter to release her, but the exit through which she could escape.

I've got to get out of here, she told herself, and reached down to tear at the knots at her feet. But her fingers bobbled weakly over the leather. Stiff and cold, they had no strength to grip and pull. She bent closer, jamming her fingertips into the knots until her nails tore and broke off at the quick. She lifted her wrists to her mouth then, and chewed at the leather with her teeth, but the thongs seemed only to tighten. Still she worked at them, thinking as she bit at the leather, trying to sort out the events of the past two days.

Her thoughts gleamed and guttered like fireflies in a summer night, without order or logic, providing only glimpses of reality—Isaac stalking across the island intent on murder, McPherson ferrying an unsuspecting Maggie to the island, Jim waiting for release or death on the cot in the cottage. Delia forced herself to slow down, to think methodically. McPherson and his father had brought Maggie to the island alone, unaccompanied by the official search party. They could have no intention of allowing her to find Jim, unless they wanted their enterprise revealed.

Galvanized by sudden understanding, Delia redoubled her efforts to tear away the leather thongs. Like the goat that leads the sheep to slaughter, McPherson was guiding Maggie to the island. He had them all together now—Maggie and Jim and Delia and Isaac—the only people other than his father and Joshua who could swear to his crimes. Sealed in the cave, they would be no more threat to him, their disappearance blamed like the others on Isaac.

By now, Maggie and the McPhersons would have reached the cottage. In the relief of their reunion, her mother and Jim would ignore caution. Snared in Mc-Pherson's trap, they would both be hostage to his plans.

Delia continued to struggle with the knots, but they did not loosen. No matter how desperate Isaac was, he could not succeed against McPherson, Mr. Mac and Joshua. Even Maggie and Jim might fight him, unaware of his innocence in the murder of the game warden. Fear tickled at the edges of her mind like the soft, sticky treading of a spider. Somehow she had to get help, to get to Isaac before his attempt at revenge destroyed him. Her tugging had tightened the loops around her wrists and ankles. Her hands and feet were numb, clumsy lumps at the ends of her arms and legs. Frustrated, Delia glanced around the cave.

Isaac had said she could move. The cave was full of shards and scraps of stone. If she could find one sharp enough, she could cut herself loose. With one foot she scraped aside a pile of stones. At her movement Rea stopped panting, licked her lips and cocked her head.

Her ears pricked forward with interest, but she remained lying on the shore of the lagoon. Delia reached down to the stones, but her fingers were too numb to sense their sharpness. Balancing against the wall, she swung her arms from side to side and wriggled her fingers, then moved her hands up and down in a chopping motion. Her fingers tingled with renewed circulation, and she began to feel warmer. She tried jogging in place, but the leather tripped her. Moving slightly away from the wall, she started a series of knee bends. As she dropped down, a hard lump jabbed into her groin. Delia gasped and straightened. Her father's knife, forgotten in her panicked flight from the island and from the storm, was there in the corner of her jeans. All she had to do was shove her bound hands far enough into her pocket to slip the knife out, and she was free.

Twisting to the side, Delia pushed her hands against the hard denim pocket seam, but could not reach the rough bone handle. She struggled for a moment, then yanked at the snap at her waist. Loosened, her jeans flapped open. The pocket bounced heavily against her hip. She grabbed the material, turned it until the knife slipped out, and caught and cradled it in her open palms. Slowly, afraid to drop the knife on the damp, uneven floor of the cave, Delia sat down and pried open the blade. She positioned the knife in one hand so that she could saw at the leather that bound her wrists. Again and again the blade slipped over the leather until at last it caught and cut. Slowly the leather parted, then snapped in two. Delia tore the thongs off and hacked through the line at her ankles. She pocketed the knife and stood up, facing the wolf.

"All right, Rea," she said, reaching out. At the sound of her name, the wolf flicked her ears and drew back her lips, swiping them with her tongue. Delia took a step forward. The wolf rose, amber eyes gleaming in the dim cavern. Still holding out her hand, Delia moved closer until Rea's nose was inches from her palm. She took a deep breath and reached over and up, slipping her hand onto the wolf's head and down through the rough fur of her neck. As Isaac had done, Delia scratched behind Rea's ears, then slowly moved to the animal's side. Rea turned her head. Delia could see the slits of Rea's nostrils open and close, and felt the shoulder muscles flex beneath her thick coat. She shivered at the thought of Rea's snapping jaws, now open and grinning back at her.

"Easy, Rea," she murmured, and took another step away. The wolf gave a low whine and flicked her tongue over her white teeth. Her ears dropped back. Delia stood still. A properly trained dog, she had read somewhere, would take a command from anyone. Isaac had trained Rea. But still, Rea was a wolf. Carefully Delia faced her.

"Down, Rea," she ordered, trying not to look at the powerful jaw, the flattened ears and wrinkled brow. "Lie down, Rea."

Rea barked, ending in a note that was something between a whine and a growl, and eased back on her haunches. Delia raised her hand and repeated the order. Hesitantly, Rea lay down on the rocky shore. Delia stepped back and the wolf sat up. Her tail twitched and her rear legs were tensed to move. Delia watched her, meeting the pale golden eyes, then decided.

"Okay, Rea. You win. If you won't stay here alone, you'll have to come along. Let's go find Isaac."

The wolf pranced forward, her tail high and bushy, her ears forward and eager. She bumped against Delia's legs, circling her, and her claws scraped on the rough stone of the shore. Delia touched the wolf's head, running her hand between Rea's ears and scratching the slope of skull behind them.

"You'd like a run in the woods, wouldn't you," she said softly. "And I'll be a lot more comfortable with you beside me than with you chasing me. Come on, let's go." She followed the edge of the lagoon to the opening between the rocks. Looking to either side, Delia could see no sign of any other person. The lake beyond the island was empty of boats. Delia stepped out through the rocky archway of the cave.

For a moment, the warm brilliance of the sun stunned her. White granite gleamed above, painful to her eyes after the dimness of the cave. The lake sparkled green and calm along the shore, lapping gently on the slabs of slate that bordered the cave entrance. With Rea at her heels, Delia started to climb the hillside, angling east toward the cottage and the dock where Maggie and the McPhersons would have come ashore.

She made no effort to be quiet. If anything, her noise 183

might distract McPherson and gain time, enough for Delia to signal the search parties that by now were out on the lake. She crashed through the brush, tugging and pulling herself up the hillside toward the crest of the island where the going would be easier. Rea left her to follow her own route. The wolf was invisible in the trees, but Delia could hear her, paralleling Delia's own course up the hill. When she reached the top, Delia paused to get her bearings.

The dipping saddle of the island was behind her, and she was standing on an outcrop of the granite cliff. Below her on the north was the shallow cave opening where she had been driven by the storm, and on the south was the entrance she had just left. Behind her on the western tip of the island was the small harbor where Isaac had moored the launch. Ahead, through the thick growth of pines, was the clearing where Lobo had died, and the shuttered back of the cottage.

Catching her breath, Delia stood on the high ground, listening, straining to hear voices or the sound of a motor from the water below. But there was nothing. The island was as quiet as it had been on the morning of her arrival. Delia looked out over the calm lake. Colored by distance, the islands loomed in greens and whites close up, fading to gray, half-imagined horizons far off. There was no sign of McPherson's white boat, no indication that he'd completed his business and left the island.

184   *They're still here*, Delia thought, and pressed on. She

ran through the woods, tripping over the leather that flapped around her ankles. She stumbled over rocks and logs as she plunged forward. Rotting branches rolled and crumbled, throwing her off balance into sun-starved, dying pine limbs and clumps of stunted brush. Moss-covered rocks sprang up under her feet. Her breath began to come in sharp jabs, punctuated by a dull ache in her side. But she kept on until at last she saw the trees thin ahead of her, marking the edge of the clearing. She forced herself to slow down and look around her for Isaac. With any luck she would find him here, before he'd made his suicidal attack. At the last ring of trees she stopped.

The rain had washed the rocks in the clearing clean of the stain of Lobo's blood. The pile of green branches Delia had gathered lay wilted, a loose fortification between her and the cottage. The building seemed abandoned, its windows still shuttered, its chimney cold and smokeless. Delia stood behind the trees and looked at the opposite sides of the clearing, watching for the green plaid of Isaac's shirt to separate itself from the cool shadows of the woods. But she saw and heard nothing, not even Rea's silvery padding.

They must be inside, Delia said to herself. *They've got to be there.* But she heard no voices, no hint that the cottage was occupied.

Maybe Isaac did surprise them, she thought. *Maybe I'm too late.* She thrust the thought aside. The important thing was to get to the fire and light it.

Delia hesitated another minute, then crouched and ran across the clearing to the pile of saplings. Her back crawled with the thought of McPherson's spotting her now, and her skin prickled at the memory of the hard, inexorable grip of his huge hands. That strength could reach out and snatch her easily from the false security of her hiding place behind the cut trees. She glanced around her, but saw nothing. Pushing closer to the wilted leaves, she smelled their damp, bruised scent. Soaked by the rain, they would dry quickly in the hot sun. The sky above her was a pure and cloudless blue. Delia patted the pocket of her Windbreaker and felt the matches still packaged there in the plastic bag. She pulled them out and shook them from the wrapper. Spreading the cut limbs of the saplings, she tunneled into the pile she'd made, finding the dry leaves she'd placed at its base.

She struck the match and held the flame to the leaves. They curled back from the heat, graying into ash until the match went out. She lit another and held it again against the tinder until the match heat burned her fingers. A wisp of smoke eddied from the leaves, and the twig on which they grew crackled into flame. Delia pulled back and watched the kindling catch and spread until a network of small flames burned beneath the layer of green saplings.

It would be easy now to wait, to slip back into the forest and hide until the patrol boats came across the bay into the channel. But if Maggie and Jim were still in the cottage, if there was any hope of stopping Isaac, she had to try.

Again she looked behind her, surveyed the edges of the clearing and saw no one. The woods remained still and quiet. Ahead of her was the cottage, the place of peace she had set out days ago to find. She took a series of deep breaths, building up oxygen as if she were about to run a long race instead of the short sprint between the burning signal fire and the cottage. She filled her lungs one final time and broke running from behind the fire. Touching the sun-warmed siding at the corner of the cottage, she pressed close to it, rubbing her cheek on the grainy, weathered shingles. At that moment she wanted only to remain there, supported and warmed by the island house. Instead she turned and looked back. The fire was burning in earnest now, and a plume of smoke rose straight up, hanging above the trees in the still air, visible beyond the channel out into the bay. If the search parties were on the lake, the smoke would bring them quickly. Somehow she had to hold McPherson off until then.

With her back to the shingles, Delia slipped along the side of the cottage to the front. She paused again, looked around the porch and saw no one. The padlocked plywood door cover was still swung back from the doorway. Delia started up the stairs, padding softly in her sneakers. As she neared the doorway, she heard the rumble of voices and the unmistakable treble of Maggie's exclamations. The sound of her mother's voice spurred her forward. She took the last two steps in a single leap, crossed the porch and shoved open the unlatched door of the cottage.

As she stepped across the threshold, the dimly lit room exploded with motion. In a jumble of colors and shadows, hands reached out, heads turned, mouths flashed white teeth in shouts of surprise and anger. Like stops in a broken film, faces registered in Delia's eyes. Maggie, small and haggard, threw herself toward the doorway, her palms up as if warding Delia off. Jim shouted, his eyes wide with dismay as he pushed himself up from the dirty cot mattress. Standing still and open-mouthed beside them, Mr. Mac touched a hand to the gray stubble of his beard, which looked like a ragged mask against the rough tan of his chin. Young McPherson swung toward her with a rifle tilted in the crook of his elbow. Beside her in the doorway was a guide, the rough wool of his green plaid shirt so close that Delia could feel the scratch of its threads on her jacket. And slumped in a chair near Jim, his face slack with disbelief, was Isaac.

"Cordelia, run!" Maggie screamed, waving her arms to brush Delia out the door. With a swipe of his forearm, young McPherson shoved her back. She tumbled into Jim's cot, falling awkwardly over his splinted leg with a cry. He paled and groaned, sagging backward on the mattress.

"Get out of here, Delia," he managed to call to her. "The boat—take the boat and go."

As he spoke, Isaac heaved himself against the chair and lunged forward into young McPherson's knees, knocking the man back into the table. The kerosene lamp rocked, tilted and crashed to the floor, exploding into yellow flames. The guide in the doorway snatched the blanket from Jim's cot to smother them, while McPherson jabbed at Isaac with the butt of the rifle. In that split second, Delia realized that Isaac was bound to the chair, held prisoner with Maggie and Jim. He twisted away from the rifle long enough to fix his eyes on Delia.

"Rea!" he hissed. "Call Rea."

The rifle hit the side of his head with a sickening thud, and he lay limp on the floor. Like nightmare creatures, Mr. Mac and his son came toward Delia, grasping for her, their hands so close that she could see the ridged, yellow nails at their fingertips. She tried to back away, but all her reflexes seemed slowed, as though she moved in the terrible slow motion of dreams, her body weighted and unresponsive, while their hands loomed larger and closer.

"Get her," she heard Mr. Mac's son shout. "And this time make sure you do."

Delia turned to run.

FOURTEEN 🌿

The old man's footsteps thudded behind her on the porch, as Delia bolted out the door and down the steps. She half fell, half ran toward the path to the dock, slipping on the pine needles that had fallen and lay undisturbed over it. Her wind was better, and she was faster than Mr. Mac, but she was hampered by shock and indecision about whether to run or to fight. He gained at her every hesitation, until, jumping over a rock, Delia snagged the loose leather around her ankle and toppled onto the needle-cushioned path. She yanked at the thong, but Mr. Mac was already on her, snatching at the hood of her parka, pinning one arm behind her as he dragged her up off the ground.

"Sorry, Delia," he wheezed as he jerked the leather free and set her on her feet. "I've got no choice."

Breathless and dismayed by the scene in the cottage, Delia responded to the pressure on her arm and let him urge her up to the steps. Clouds of smoke were rising now above the island from Delia's signal fire in the clearing. Acrid smoke filled the air. Mr. Mac sniffed, his nostrils wrinkling, and looked at the sky.

"Your idea, I suppose," he growled, shoving Delia ahead of him. "They'll see it, all right, the search party. We'll have to work fast."

He hurried her up the stairs. The smoke was thicker here, filled with the oily smell of kerosene. Threads of black ash fluttered onto the deck on a wave of hot air. As Delia and Mr. Mac came abreast of the door, they felt a surge of heat. Yellow flames licked across the hardwood floor inside the cottage, spreading out from the dark, greasy stain of the kerosene. They burst up inches above the floor, as though the air itself were the flammable substance and would catch and burn at random. The guide had given up his efforts to suffocate the blaze. The blanket lay to one side, burning and spreading the fire to the carefully draped furniture. Shards of the broken lamp lay among the flames, blackening with soot. Fanned by the cooler air being drawn in the kitchen window, the fire grew and exhaled its increasing heat at the doorway. McPherson stood there, his huge shoulders blocking the opening. He was pulling on the bound bundle of furs while the guide shoved at it from the other end, and with his free hand McPherson wielded the rifle, fending off Maggie's desperate attacks.

"You're not going anywhere, lady," he shouted over the rush of flames. And then to the guide, "Get those furs out!"

But the heat was too intense. The flames were reaching

two and three feet from the floor, brushing the guide's pants and shirt. Sparks rose into the air and came down on his face and in his hair. He dropped his end of the furs, shoved his way past McPherson and, beating at his face and head, vaulted over the porch railing and ran down toward the water. Turning to stop him, McPherson saw Delia and his father. He grabbed her arm.

"Get her in there," he called to Mr. Mac. His hand was like an iron band around Delia's upper arm. But Mr. Mac held back.

"No," he shouted at his son. "Let them out. She's signaled the rangers. You can't do this. We'll be caught."

McPherson turned toward him, his face wet with sweat and streaked with the black ash of the fire. "Get her in with the rest of them."

"It's too late," the old man wailed. "The rangers will be here. They'll know."

"You want to burn, too?" McPherson demanded, brandishing the rifle.

Mr. Mac let go of Delia, shying away from the rifle barrel. But the younger man was too quick for him. He swung Delia aside and clipped Mr. Mac across the side of the head with the rifle, knocking him to his knees on the deck. Then he forced Delia forward into the cottage.

The room was filled with smoke now, so that only shapes were visible in the yellow flickering of the flames. Maggie was on her knees beside the cot, coughing, holding a corner of her shirt over her mouth. Jim was

192

half off the cot, hanging close to the floor beside her to escape the smoke. Near them, his eyes open now, Isaac lay, still tied to the wooden chair. The fire was only inches from his face, and he drew his head back from the heat.

"Don't do it," Delia heard Mr. Mac shouting behind her. "They'll get us. It's too late."

She dug in her heels at the threshold, but McPherson easily pressed her ahead of him. As she stumbled forward she screamed, and screaming, remembered Rea. With her last clear breath she began to howl, summoning up a shattering baying from her primitive desire to survive. And then the smoke was in her lungs, cutting off not only the sound, but air itself. She strangled, coughed and slipped to her knees. McPherson had pulled over the plywood door and was jamming it against her, forcing her farther into the oven of the cottage, pushing the solid wood closed behind her. She could hear the clink of the padlock as he reached for it, to secure the latch. The light dimmed and the flames sprang up in front of her. She pressed her body against the door, trying to wedge herself into the last narrow crease of its opening, and suddenly it gave way. Delia fell backward onto the deck at McPherson's feet.

Like a company of demons, Rea's howls had broken out in answer to Delia's desperate effort. The wolf was running toward the cottage now, through the long grass, up the needle-strewn path to the steps of the deck. Her body gleamed in the smoky air as she sprang forward. Mr. Mac lay on the deck, stunned by his son's blow. 193

McPherson had released his pressure on the door to meet the wolf's charge. He raised his rifle and aimed it as she bounded toward him from the bottom steps of the deck.

Delia saw the wolf leap into the air. Rea seemed to hang there, her body stretched full length for the attack. Her ears were back, her jaws open and bared, her legs reaching toward the big man's chest. McPherson met her with the rifle, swinging it in perfect line with her silvery body. He braced himself. Delia could see his intake of breath, his pressure on the trigger. She felt herself scream, but heard no sound. The wolf hurtled through the air, a gray ghost of snarling motion. Delia heard the trigger click, and Rea hit McPherson full in the chest with the gathered force of her weight and spring. He staggered backward and fell, and she was on him, tearing at the rough wool of his shirt as he pressed his forearms over his face and neck, and beat at the wolf's jaws. McPherson was calling for help, but Delia ignored him. She left him rolling with Rea on the deck, teetering in combat at its edge. Rea's teeth slashed and snapped, and her snarls blended with Mc-Pherson's panting as he fought her.

Delia could hear the crackle of flames from the interior of the cottage. The fire was building, and its roar challenged the noise of the man's struggle with the wolf. Pulling her jacket over her face, Delia threw herself face down on the floor and snaked her way toward the cot where Maggie and Jim had been.

194   "Get out of here, Delia," Maggie gasped as Delia

grasped her arm and began to pull. But Delia hung onto her and continued to pull, tugging and shoving her mother toward the fresh air. When she saw that Maggie had made it to the doorway she turned to Jim. The splint on his leg was torn loose, and he lay barely conscious, half on and half off the cot. Delia wriggled away from him through the smoke and heat to Isaac's chair. She hacked away the rope that tied him, shoving the chair back from the flames. At last he was free. Coughing and choking, they crawled to Jim's side, hoisted him on their shoulders and staggered out onto the deck.

"Rea," Delia croaked as the cool air filled her lungs and she could speak again. "Call Rea."

McPherson had held the wolf off, but his defense was weakening. Rea stood over him, snarling, her huge paws on his shoulders holding him down, while she snapped and tore at his flailing arms.

"Down, Rea," Isaac commanded in a calm and even voice. "Get back. Down."

The wolf eased away from the supine man, snarling. She stood at McPherson's feet, still growling, her tail low and her ears down, her lips wrinkled in suspicion. Slowly McPherson propped himself up on his elbows.

"The rifle misfired," he said. "It must have. I couldn't have missed."

Before he could reach for the weapon, Isaac kicked it aside, away from McPherson and toward the flaming doorway of the cottage. McPherson's wool shirt was shredded at the neck and shoulders, and his face was badly scratched. Long, deep gashes marked his fore- 195 arms, bleeding heavily, but he would survive. The wolf watched him with narrow, yellow eyes, her growl rumbling low in her throat. Beside Jim on the deck, Mr. Mac sat stunned. On the shore below, the guide emerged from the lake, the sparks in his clothes extinguished. He glanced up the hill, then ran down the pier and jumped into McPherson's boat. In moments he had started the motor.

"Stop him," McPherson shouted. "He's got the boat. He's getting away."

"Not for long," Isaac said, watching the boat skim toward the channel. "The patrol boats will pick him up." Then he turned to Delia. "Get everyone off this porch. The fire will reach here next."

Together Maggie and Delia helped Jim into the shade of a pine tree at the head of the path. Safe from the blaze, they were able to watch the channel for approaching boats while Isaac and Rea herded McPherson and Mr. Mac away from the fire. Under Rea's guard they made no effort to escape.

"Listen, Miss Maggie," Mr. Mac appealed to her, trying to explain. "You have to listen to me. I never meant for it to get this far. There wasn't supposed to be any killing. It was just a plan to make a little extra money. Lord knows I needed it. I didn't mean any harm. You've got to believe me."

"I don't have to believe anything," Maggie said, bending over Jim's leg to replace the splint. "You can make your explanations to the authorities."

"If only you'd stayed away, there'd have been no problem," the old man insisted. "Nobody was supposed to get hurt. Why, if I'd had any idea that Delia would go out in that raft in the storm, I'd never have let them cut the nozzle."

Maggie looked up at him. "You can stand there and tell me you meant no harm when Delia could have drowned because of you?" Her hands trembled as she tied the splint.

"It was a slow leak," Delia said. "Just enough to get me into deep water."

Maggie sprang up and hugged Delia to her. "Thank God you're all right!" She smoothed her hand across Delia's face and hair, tracing a scratch on Delia's cheek with her cool, thin fingertips. "Let me look at you. Are you really all right?"

For the first time Delia considered what she must look like. Her pants legs were torn and muddy, hanging in tatters around her ankles. Her parka was pulled and ripped at the elbows and shoulders, with brambles still hanging from it. Her hair was a wild tangle of curls, damp with sweat, and her hands and arms were covered with dirt and scratches.

"I'm okay, I guess."

"You'd have been fine if you'd stayed where you belonged," Mr. Mac said, still trying to get Maggie's attention. "You've got to understand that it's not my fault."

"Then whose fault is it?" Maggie turned on him. "I   197

suppose that isn't your fault?" She pointed to the cottage. Flames were licking around the door and out the kitchen window. Black smoke rose from the building, meeting and blending with the smoke from Delia's signal fire. But the fresh, clean scent of cut, burning wood was obliterated by the oily billowing from the cottage, still tinged with the odor of kerosene. Heat shimmered in waves over the roof, and small tongues of fire appeared between the shingle siding of the walls. The air heaved and rushed around the cottage. With a burst, flames broke through the roof, and a blast of heat rolled back over the small group gathered on the hill.

"Delia," Maggie murmured, reaching out to her daughter. "Delia, I'm so sorry."

She pulled Delia into her arms, pressing the girl's face into her shoulder so that she could not see the hot and raging force that engulfed the building. Gratefully, Delia leaned against her, suddenly tired, glad to close out the present against the slim support of Maggie's shoulder.

"I am sorry," Maggie repeated. "This wasn't what I wanted. Not this. Even if we hadn't kept the place, I wouldn't have wanted this."

"I know," Delia mumbled.

"All your father's work," Maggie said, staring over Delia's head at the flames. Her whole body trembled, and she tightened her arms around Delia. Gently she eased her daughter away from the fire, down onto the path. "Except for you, Jim and I would still be in there."

"It was Isaac. I couldn't have done it without Isaac."

"At least we're safe, all of us." Again Delia felt the shudder in her mother's thin frame. "I was so frightened."

"Me, too," Delia said in a small voice. Comforted in Maggie's arms, she had no need of the anger that had separated them for so long, and no desire to summon it up.

"I mean, when I discovered you were missing, too," Maggie explained. She pushed back a little from Delia so that she could look into her face. "When I got up in the morning and found you were gone, I didn't know what to do."

Delia dropped her eyes, looking at the grass at their feet. The night she had slipped away seemed centuries ago, and certainly had no part in this moment on her island.

"First Jim, and then you. . . ."

"And Daddy," Delia said quickly. "First Daddy."

"Yes," Maggie nodded. "Your father." She tilted Delia's head up with a finger under her chin, forcing her daughter to look at her. "Didn't you know what you were doing to me?"

"I wasn't doing anything to you," Delia protested. Like sandpaper, Maggie's question rubbed on her raw nerves. "I was doing something for me. I had to come here."

"But Delia, if we'd never found you, what would I have done?"

"You'd have had Jim."

"Jim is my husband. You're my daughter."

Delia backed out of her mother's arms. "And you'd rather be with him. I don't blame you, really. It's easier when I'm not around. So I came here. And I can stay here. I can take care of myself."

"Cordelia!" Maggie gripped her shoulders hard. "Now that I have you back, do you think I'd leave you here?"

"I'm just a reminder to you, of things you'd rather forget. You want to start over."

"Not without you." Maggie held onto her, her fingers tightening in spite of Delia's resistance. "It's not the same with Jim as it was with your father. It can't be and shouldn't be. He's a whole new person, separate from you, and separate from me. You're my daughter."

"And I'm not separate?"

Maggie smiled. "I've been thinking that we're like these islands, Delia, that stand alone or seem to be part of one another, depending on your perspective. Sometimes we're separate and sometimes we're not. If I'd lost you now, before we'd learned to appreciate our differences, we'd never have had the distance to become friends again."

"I had to come here," Delia said again, pulling out of Maggie's hands to stand alone in front of her. "To remember. I had to come back to the island."

Maggie nodded. "I did, too, but I didn't know it."

"Then don't criticize me for it. You couldn't have come—you wouldn't be here now—if I hadn't run away."

"When I thought you were gone, Delia," Maggie said quietly, "when I thought you were lost on the lake in your raft, I began thinking and I realized I'd been wrong about a lot of things. Starting over the way I did was wrong. And hanging onto you and Jim the way I did, so that I was always between you, was wrong. I didn't trust you or myself enough to let us be separate. After your father died, I couldn't just go on." The words wobbled, but Maggie didn't pause. "I couldn't just continue. I had to start over, completely over, I thought, and this time I was determined to hang on so that I'd never lose like that again." Maggie dropped her hands to her sides. "But sometimes the way to hold on is to let go. I had to learn that. I won't always remember it, but I have learned it."

"And what if what you had is gone when you look for it?" Delia asked, feeling the hot weight of the cottage burning behind her. "What then?"

Maggie shook her head. "I'm not sure I know the answer to that. You remember, I guess, and grieve."

Their eyes met, and held. "That's the first honest answer you've given me since Daddy died," Delia said.

"It's the first honest question you've asked," Maggie replied, smiling away any sting to her words. "I'm just glad to have you safely back, Delia, both you and Jim." Reaching out, she hugged Delia again and looked over to where Jim lay on the grass.

Delia straightened and stepped back. They were safe now, all of them, but had anything really changed?

Maggie and Jim were reunited, but Delia was alone, without even the sanctuary of the island to come to. She turned toward Isaac, who stood apart from the others, his back to her, looking out over the water. Separate, she corrected herself, separate but not necessarily alone. In the afternoon sun, the waters of Ghost Bay were smooth and green, angling down into blackness. Isaac raised his hand and pointed. Coming into the channel at high speed were two boats—government boats following the signal of the smoke.

❧FIFTEEN

The boats bellied up to the dock in the deep wash of their wakes, and the officers disembarked. They ran up the path, shouting to one another about the fire, and stopped at the sight of the people rimming the burning cottage.

"What's going on here?" Constable Allyn asked. Seeing Rea poised over McPherson, still threatening with her low growls, he drew his pistol. "Don't move, anybody, it may be rabid," he ordered.

"Wait, don't shoot!" Delia stepped between the gun and Rea. Facing Allyn, she backed toward the wolf, reaching out until she felt the rough fur of Rea's heavy coat under her palm. "She won't hurt anyone."

"Delia, get away from that animal," Maggie gasped. "What do you mean, she won't hurt anyone? Look at Mr. McPherson."

"It's all right, Mom. She won't hurt me. She belongs to Isaac."

203

"And he's the one you're after," McPherson told the rangers. "Arrest that man. He tried to kill us. He's the renegade you're after, the one who killed the game warden. Arrest him."

"No," Delia cried, turning on McPherson. "Not Isaac. You."

McPherson ignored her and staggered to his feet. "He sicked that wolf on me when I was trying to help these people. Their cottage was on fire. He's dangerous, I tell you."

"That's a lie." Winding her fingers in the wolf's thick fur, Delia stood face to face with McPherson. Streaked with dirt and soot from the fire, and with the blood from his fresh wounds, he was hardly a convincing villain. "You're the one who's been poaching on the lake, you and Mr. Mac. You nearly drowned me, and you'd have locked us all in the cottage to burn if it hadn't been for Rea."

Allyn glanced from Delia to McPherson to Isaac. "Aren't you Isaac—Isaac Smith?"

Isaac looked quickly behind him at the woods, at the thick shadows and brush that could hide him if he slipped away. Like the animals he'd lived with for so long, he did not trust the men around him. These were the enemy who had turned away his reports and accused him of the crimes he'd tried to stop. These were the men who enforced the rules that changed his land and shook his people from it. He tensed, poised on his toes, his bruised knuckles clenched at his sides. His eyes slid to Delia, still standing with her hand in Rea's fur, held for an instant, and then looked back at the constable.

"Yes, I'm Isaac."

"And that's your wolf?"

"I raised her from a pup, yes."

"About time we caught up with you," Allyn said.

"Right," McPherson crowed. "Get him off this lake and behind bars, and you'll have no more trouble."

"No," Delia cried. "Isaac saved my life—Isaac and Rea. It's McPherson you should arrest. He tried to kill us all."

"You're hysterical, little lady. I was just trying to put the fire out."

"She's about as hysterical as I am," Jim spoke up. His voice was hoarse from the smoke, but strong. "These men attacked my family," he said to the constable. "I want them arrested."

"You're delirious, Mr. Marshall. It's the pain."

"I didn't spend three days in that cottage with your guide holding a rifle on me without picking up some interesting facts. I'll press charges against you, McPherson, and make them stick if it takes the rest of my life."

Injured as he was, Jim was there, backing Delia up. He looked worn and tired, but no less determined for that. Under the three days' growth of beard, his chin was set.

"And as for this man," he said, indicating Isaac, "if anything, he deserves a medal."

"He's likely to get it," Allyn said, shoving his pistol

into its holster and holding out his hand to Isaac, "for helping an officer in trouble. I want to thank you for what you did. If we hadn't found Charlie on the dock when we did, he wouldn't have made it. There's one less casualty in the ranks, thanks to you."

"Davis is all right?" Isaac asked.

"He will be. His fractures have to heal, but he remembered your finding him out on the bay and bringing him in to Government Docks. You can bet he set us straight when we told him there was a warrant out for you."

"He must have been out of his head," McPherson insisted. "You know what kind of a reputation Isaac has on this lake."

"Charlie Davis doesn't make mistakes," the trooper said, looking coldly at McPherson. "Not since he made the mistake of trusting you when he stopped your boat. That was very nearly fatal."

"I don't know what you're talking about."

"You had a boatload of illegal skins that night, Mr. McPherson, all headed across the border to those collectors who've got nothing better to do with their money."

"Prove it."

"Charlie will swear to it."

"He was in a coma long enough to forget whatever he thinks he saw. No court would convict me on his testimony."

"They won't have to," Delia said. She smiled grimly at McPherson. "There are stacks of furs right there—

all the proof anybody needs. Jim saw them, and my mother, and so did I. That whole bundle of furs is proof."

She turned, pointing toward the cottage, which still flamed against the early evening sky. McPherson laughed, the icy crackling Delia had heard off Cat Point on the morning of Jim's disappearance.

"It was all there in your cottage, little lady, and all gone up in smoke. And even if you salvaged some of it, what would it prove? You and your good friend Isaac could have been in this business together. It's your island."

Delia's smile sagged, then she raised her head and set her chin. With Jim and Maggie and the game warden behind her and Isaac, McPherson would be convicted. "No one would believe that," she said to him. "Besides, there's the cave."

"There's plenty of evidence there," Isaac agreed.

"You found it?" Mr. Mac asked. "You were in the cave?"

"Shut up, old man," McPherson bellowed at him.

"I'm through shutting up." Mr. Mac sighed, rubbed the bruised lump on his head and cleared his throat. "Time we settled this whole thing."

"Don't listen to him," McPherson interrupted. "He's nothing but a worn-out old bum. He doesn't know what he's saying. Folks around here know about his stories."

"They don't know this one."

"I said shut up." McPherson lunged at the older man, 207

but Constable Allyn stepped between them and shouldered McPherson aside.

"Isaac never had anything to do with this," Mr. Mac said. He gestured toward Maggie and Delia. "It's really your fault he got involved at all, talking to him the way you did, treating him like he was a member of the family. If you hadn't convinced him he had something to say about what happened on this lake, he'd have kept his nose out of my business."

"The lake is my business," Isaac said. "It was always my business."

"Then you got what you asked for. I warned you. I told you not to make waves with the guests, but you lectured them anyway. And I told you to forget the poaching. You could have overlooked those traps you found."

"They were out of season. They were illegal and you had no right setting them. Davis and I would have stopped you then if we'd known about the cave. I thought I'd searched every inch of this island."

"You should have let me do things my way." McPherson lurched toward his father again.

"It was your idea to set him up with that fishing party. That didn't get rid of him."

"The party that disappeared?" Allyn asked. "You did that?"

"Did what?" Mr. Mac turned away from his son. "Nothing happened to those men. They weren't even tourists. They were clients."

"You mean they aren't dead?"

"As far as I know they're safe in the States, looking for more shipments. And you played right into it," Mr. Mac said, sneering at Isaac. "It was your own fault, really, that you had it so rough. The way you acted toward the tourists—who wouldn't believe you'd massacre them, given half a chance."

"What I don't understand," Maggie said to the old man, "is why you took our reservation in the first place."

"It was a good cover," Mr. Mac answered. "If I'd known it was you, things would have been different. But I needed the money."

"That's what started all the trouble," Jim said. "The resort was losing money. McPherson came up here expecting to take over a lucrative tourist business. Instead he discovered that his father was nearly bankrupt. So he decided on another way to get rich."

"But once you knew we were here," Delia asked, "why didn't you clear the furs out?"

"We were trying to." McPherson glared at Jim. "And we'd have finished the job if he hadn't gone for a walk and stumbled onto us. I should have taken care of him when I had the chance. I'd have gotten rid of you all if it hadn't been for that wolf."

Delia remembered Rea's leap, the wolf hurtling through the air, the click of the rifle, and McPherson driven down on the porch by Rea's weight.

"Your rifle never fired," she said. "It was no good after you shot Lobo."

"That's nonsense," McPherson snarled. "Just some of your stupid Indian superstition."

"But Rea's alive." Isaac looked at the wolf sitting quietly beneath the stroking of Delia's hand. "Your rifle's gone."

The flames were burning now across the deck of the cottage, leaping up where Isaac had kicked the rifle, crawling up the railing and down the steps in tongues of orange and yellow. The building was gone, the furs, the rifle burned. The carefully boarded and locked contents of the cottage were nothing but ashes. There was a silence as everyone watched the fire finish its destruction. Then Delia turned away, unable to look any longer at the charred gray remains.

"There is a reward, Delia," Constable Allyn said, coming over to her. "I know it's not much consolation, but by rights it belongs to you. The newspapers offered a reward for information leading to the arrest of the game warden's murderer."

"It belongs to Isaac. He's the one who stopped them."

"Seems to me it was a joint effort, but you can do what you want. I'll see that the right people are notified."

"We really have to get these people to a doctor," Maggie said, approaching the constable. "There's nothing more we can do here. Can you take us to the mainland?"

"Yes, ma'am. We'll radio for an ambulance to meet us in Sioux Narrows." Allyn turned to his partners. "Get them in the boat," he ordered, indicating McPherson and Mr. Mac. "Then come back and help me get Mr. Marshall down this hill."

"What will happen to them?" Delia asked, watching the men move down the hill to the government boat.

"The courts will take care of them now," Jim said. "They'll be lenient with the old man, though I expect he will lose the resort. The fact that he's willing to testify against the others is in his favor."

Jim leaned back against the tree and closed his eyes, breathing deeply.

"Your leg, is it worse?" Delia asked.

Jim opened his eyes and looked at her. "Not really. It doesn't feel good, but it's no worse. I was thinking about the cottage. I am sorry, Delia."

"Thanks. It wasn't your fault."

"That's not quite true. If I'd realized how much all this meant to you, if I'd taken the time to ask. . . ." He stopped. "We'd have done things differently, that's all."

"Nobody will want to buy it now."

"Do you want to sell it?"

"Do I have a choice?"

"I think you should. You've got a mind of your own."

Delia looked closely at him, to see if he was making fun of her. "I didn't know you'd noticed."

He smiled. "I've noticed a lot in the last few days that I wasn't able to see before."

"Because of my mother, you mean?"

"And because of myself."

"I think she was afraid you wouldn't like me."

"Or that you wouldn't like me."

Delia considered that. "I never thought of it that way, my not liking you."

"I wouldn't blame you if you didn't. Your father was a very special person. It can't be easy for you to have me where he always was."

"That's not your fault, either."

"Just the same, it could get in the way of our being friends."

Delia looked away, down the hill toward the dock. It made her uncomfortable to talk to Jim this way. It was easier to pretend he was a guest, a casual visitor to whom she only had to be polite. But that was as unreal as trying to pretend that her father had just gone out fishing. She glanced at her stepfather, not quite meeting his eyes, but acknowledging his existence.

"I guess it could at that. But I'll try not to let it," she said.

"That's all I could ask for, Delia." Jim reached up and touched her hand, squeezing her fingers gently. "Thanks."

❊SIXTEEN

They carried Jim down to the dock in a stretcher made of blankets and oars from the pump house. Even with his leg cushioned, the trip to the boat was painful. His face was pale, and drops of perspiration beaded on his forehead as he lay back on the boat deck.

"Is he all right?" Delia asked, watching Maggie adjust some life jackets around Jim's leg to buffer it during the ride across the bay.

"He will be," Maggie answered, "as soon as we get a doctor to set the break. You don't look too well yourself. I want the doctor to check you out after all you've been through. Come on. Get in."

"And Isaac," Delia said. "The doctor should check him, too. That was a bad knock on the head McPherson gave him."

Maggie glanced up the hill. "I don't see him. Where is he?"

Delia turned around, scanning the dock and the path into the woods. "I'll bet he went back for the launch. You go ahead, Mom. Isaac and I will meet you at Government Docks."

"I'd rather you stayed with us," Maggie said, frowning.

"Mom, I'm all right. A little bruised, maybe," she said quickly, answering Maggie's raised eyebrows, "but I'm all right, really. I'll find Isaac and we'll come back in the launch."

"But suppose you can't find him? Suppose the fire spreads? You'd have no way off the island."

"And suppose the sun goes out, or the North Star?" Delia replied. "We'd have no way off the earth. Come on, Mom."

Maggie looked at her for a moment, then smiled. "I suppose if that did happen, we'd just have to light them again." She paused and her smile faded. "You will be careful, Delia?"

"Sure, Mom. I'll see you on the mainland."

Delia watched, waving from the dock as the government boats pulled out into the channel, the water swelling in white streaks behind them. In contrast, the water around the island was darkening, reflecting the evening sky. Mackerel clouds streaked the western horizon and caught the setting sun, changing from a gleaming gold to softer shades of peach and purple. Soon it would be dark. She went to find Isaac.

The area around the cottage was quiet—the silence of the coming night complete except for the sibilant hiss of the fire's dying embers. Delia passed the ruins of the building, drawing back from the heat as she went toward the clearing at the crest of the island. Isaac was there with Rea, on the rocks where Lobo had fallen.

"I thought you'd left," he said.

"I had some unfinished business," she answered, and watched his eyes spark with the memory of the last business they had shared.

"I should have taken you with me. But I thought I was going to kill him."

"McPherson? I was afraid you'd try."

"There didn't seem to be much reason not to. My life for his—it seemed a fair exchange."

In the shadows of the coming evening, the sharp angles of Isaac's face were softened. Delia was struck by how battered he was, thin and streaked with dirt and the scratches of his encounter with McPherson. There was a lump on his cheekbone where McPherson's rifle had hit him. Already it was turning blue, puffy and streaked with red, closing his left eye. In addition to the bruises on his face, his knuckles were scraped and his wrists were gouged red by the rope that had tied him to the chair.

"It wouldn't have been an exchange," Delia said. "There were three of them to your one. You didn't have much chance."

"I'd have done it. McPherson was standing by the door. All I had to do was grab him. I could have throttled him with my bare hands."

"But you didn't."

215

"I couldn't." Slowly he stretched out his hand and touched the thick ruff of fur at Rea's shoulders. "Nothing was that simple anymore. It wasn't just McPherson and I. There was Rea, too, and the lake, and you, waiting in the cave. I couldn't do it. As much as I hate him and what he's done, I couldn't kill him."

"I was afraid you'd get killed." Delia paused and then added, "and I was thinking of myself. I was afraid you'd leave me there, that no one would ever find me."

"I was thinking only of myself, too, Delia. I wanted you out of my way so I could do what I wanted to believe I had to do. And that was all wrong. I should have taken you with me."

"If you had, we might all have ended up in there." Delia looked back at the cottage.

"If I had, that might never have happened. I'm sorry, Delia. I should have let you help. I should have trusted you."

"I didn't give you much reason to."

"It wouldn't have mattered if you had. No one has had ears for my voice for so long, I'd forgotten anyone could."

"Except Rea."

"Except Rea and Lobo. Everyone I knew believed McPherson's lies."

"They'll listen to you now."

"Perhaps. For a while." He stood quietly by Rea in the thickening shadow.

216   "What will you do?"

"There'll be work for me here on the lake. Enough to make a living, I think."

"You could work for the Wildlife Service. And with the reward money, you could go back to school."

"You think I could stick it out this time?"

Delia looked down at the rock. "That was unfair of me. And it wasn't true. I'm sorry I said it. You had other things you had to do. But now, with the money, you could go back. And you've got a reason to stay."

"And you could rebuild the cottage with the money."

Delia held her breath for a long moment and concentrated on the sudden sparks of fireflies in the twilight. She cleared her throat. "We won't come back, Isaac, not to stay on the island. That's all gone now."

"Then I'm even sorrier for my part in it." He paused and looked out over the vast expanse of water and islands, darkening into a single horizon in the fading light. "What you said is true, Delia, in the cave. I don't want the lake to change. But it will. It has to."

"You can still protect it. Going back to school would help you do that."

"I don't know." Isaac hesitated. "There's Rea. What would I do with her?"

Delia reached out to the wolf and scratched the heavy head. "She could stay here, if you think she'd find enough food."

"With the surplus of deer here in the winter?" Isaac smiled, a complete, true smile that dizzied Delia with its warmth and lightened his face. "Even Rea could bring

217

down enough game here to keep herself fat all winter," he said. "And when the other wolves come down from the north over the ice, she'll find herself a mate. This is a good place to den. By next year she'll probably have a family. And I'll be here in the summer to watch out for them."

"You could stay on the island," Delia suggested softly.

"You're going to keep it, then?"

"I'd like to keep it for Rea, for her pups, for the wolves you want to bring back to the lake." She hesitated. But in the deepening light of evening, veiled by the soft shadows, it was easier to reach out to him. "Will you share it with me, Isaac? The island and the wolves?"

His dark eyes swung over to hers.

"Already I owe you too much, Delia. I owe you my life."

"That just makes us even." She continued to stroke the wolf's silvery fur. "It's Rea we both owe. Let me do it for her."

"McPherson nearly destroyed her," Isaac said. "He nearly destroyed all of us."

Delia could feel Rea's moist breath on her bare wrist, and the warmth of her body through the thick pelt. It was that vibrant beauty and strength that McPherson had so wantonly plundered on the lake.

"He shot her," Delia said. "He couldn't have missed. But it didn't kill her."

"Maybe the gun did misfire. Or Joshua loaded it

218

wrong. Or Rea knocked it aside when she leaped on McPherson."

"But you don't believe that."

"He'd already killed one wolf with that gun. It should have been cleaned before it was used again. Or destroyed."

Isaac was silent then. After a moment he stepped to one side, and left Delia and Rea together on the white rock. Slowly he unsheathed his knife and held it out. The blade caught the last rays of the sun and shivered with their light, sharp and deadly. Gripping the handle in both hands, Isaac raised the knife above his head. He held it there for an instant, then struck it down with all his strength against the gleaming granite rock, where the sunlight washed over the unseen stains of Lobo's blood. The blade bit into the rock, trembled and broke.

"Your knife!" Delia gasped.

"It's of no use to me now," Isaac said. "For too long I've lived by it. Its value died with Lobo."

He knelt and picked up the broken pieces, stood and threw them from the crest of the island out over the lake. The blade spun gleaming over the water, then dropped with a splash beneath the surface. Delia and Isaac watched until the circle of ripples spread and disappeared, leaving the lake smooth and calm.

Delia reached in her pocket, fingered the rough bone handle of her father's knife and drew it slowly out on her palm. She stretched her hand out to Isaac.

"You returned it once to me. It isn't a replacement,   219

but it will be a reminder of this place while you're away from it."

Isaac waited, looking at her.

"I hope it serves you well."

His hand closed over it then, touching Delia's palm lightly. "It will be a reminder and a talisman for us both. I'll return it to you—when you come back to Ghost Island."

The last streaks of sunset dimmed, blurring the boundaries of earth and sky, erasing the border between night and day. With Rea beside them, Delia and Isaac crossed the darkening island to the western shore where the launch was moored. Leaving the wolf in the sanctuary of her new home, they boarded the boat and set their course for the mainland. Circling the island, they passed the cave entrance, no more than a black cleft in the shoreline. The embers of the dying fire glowed like a gold reflection of the pale granite spine of the island. In black silhouette, the island rose against the evening sky. As Delia and Isaac drew away from it into the channel, its outlines faded and blended with the true shoreline of the lake. And rising above it into the still night came Rea's solitary howl, the music of her baying merging in harmony with that of the great lake.

You'll fall in love with these new

Laurel-Leaf romances!

MODEL BEHAVIOR
by John McNamara
Shortly after the disappearance of his idol—a pretty teenage model who was in town on a commercial shoot—Dave Callahan begins to wonder: Why does the new girl at school look so familiar?

LOVE STORY: TAKE THREE
by Gloria Miklowitz
Now that Valerie's landed a part in a TV pilot, everyone treats her like a big success. But Valerie just wants to be a normal teenager, especially with her new boyfriend Tom, who's still in the dark about Valerie's career. Can Valerie fall in love with Tom and still keep her secret?

For a complete listing of these titles, plus many more, write to us at the address below and we will send you the Dell Readers Service Listing.

DELL READERS SERVICE LISTING
P.O. Box 1045
South Holland, Illinois 60473

Dell